THE
SHIFTER BACHELOR

THE SHIFTER BACHELOR: A RARE AND UNKNOWN SHIFTER ROMANCE
Book 1

This is a work of fiction. Names, characters, places, and incidents either are the product of the author's imagination or are used fictitiously. Any resemblance to actual persons, living or dead, events, or locales is entirely coincidental.

Book Cover Design by Sanja Gombar – Fantasybookcoverdesgin.com
Cover Model & Photography – Ronnie Rogers
Edited by Elizabeth Anne Lance

First Edition: October 2018
ISBN: 978-1-7339018-0-2
ASIN: B07HTJSGVZ

Published by
Three Fortnights Press
P. O. Box 168401
Irving, TX 75016
Submissions.34Press@gmail.com

THE SHIFTER BACHELOR

A RARE AND UNKNOWN SHIFTER ROMANCE

Shai August

OTHER WORKS BY SHAI AUGUST

The Bachelor Series
The Shifter Bachelor
The Shifter Bachelorette
Bachelorette in Heat
Bachelor in Trouble
Bachelorette on a Mission – Coming October 2019
Bachelor in Paradise – Coming December 2019

Between the Numbers
The Crutchfields and The McNamaras
Trouble Ex Machina

Shorts
The After Market, Volume 1
Social Aid & Pleasure
Camp Pounce

Anthologies
Shifted Into Love: Hotel California

Table of Contents

Prologue

*I*t had been six, long arduous months since the fifty, discreetly worded nomination requests were surreptitiously delivered to the gilded mailboxes of the upper echelon of Shifter Society. Those heavily engraved invitations caused the biggest buzz in shifter society in two generations. Only one thing was asked for – Nominate one unmarried and unmated shifter lady of good birth and breeding to meet an unmated and unmarried Alpha Male of the same for compatibility and a more formal matchmaking.

Instinct told her this was the moment.

It had taken three weeks of vigorous snooping to find out who that unmated Alpha Male was, but she had succeeded. She had called in dozens of favors and promised dozens more and given a large deposit of cash to snag one of the coveted nomination forms.

A ghostly mirror image of the heavily embossed vellum paper she had sunk a full three months of magic into hovered over a hexagon shaped silver tray on the corner of her glass topped desk. Every so often she could feel the pulsing of one of the several dozen spells she had cast under the auspices of the blood moon working subtly toward her one goal.

As she had for the last few months, she resisted the urge to direct more magic at the mirror image, knowing more magic would call unwanted attention. She would get her way with patience and subtlety; of this she was certain. The nebulous plan of her last several decades was coming to fruition quicker and better than she could have anticipated.

Her cell phone hissed, and the glass desktop shook under the hardness of the phone's vibrations. One red tipped, black polished fingernail swiped the screen. She didn't say a word; the silence was prompt enough for whoever was calling to relay their message. All the breathy voice on the phone said was, "I was selected."

The call disconnected.

She flicked her hand over the top of her desk, whisking the papers away and calling her crystal ball instead.

She had more plans to put into place. Success was in her grasp now and she could feel the solidity of it forming in both her hands and her mind. Her first true smile of the last decade appeared as she began scrying for future pitfalls to her success.

Chapter One

Not So Instant Attraction

Imani paused in the doorway and inhaled deeply. She let the scents of the room's occupants filter through her nose. "All I smell is fur and shea butter," Imani whispered to her best friend through the Bluetooth headset tucked into her small ear. She stood in the doorway a moment longer and inhaled deeply again. "Yeah, not a feather, scale, or hide in evidence."

"That can't be good. It's just too early in the morning. You know some shifters are very late risers," Davida said as she yawned loudly for emphasis. "I mean if I wasn't used to your early morning calls since fifth or sixth grade, I would probably still be in bed."

"Like, you aren't in bed now?" Imani chuckled. She could hear the rustle of Davida's sheets through the phone. Davida might take her early morning calls, but her inner lioness made sure they were still in bed and they would go right back to sleep after talking to Imani.

She sighed and strode toward the coffee kiosk, a metal cart with large wheels painted purple. The spokes of the wheel alternated between steely grey and black. The scent of fresh brewed Columbian coffee was her own personal early morning oasis in the large rectangular dining hall of Wiley College. The small kiosk was blessedly free of a line at just moments before six a.m.

"How can I help you, Professor?" the petite shifter asked cheerily. The barista was blessed with the most striking blue-black skin Imani had ever seen. Her short, spiky electric blue mohawk only complimented her skin.

"I'm not a professor, but I'll take the largest, strongest coffee you have with seven creams and seven sugars," Imani answered smiling. Being this polite before coffee was killing her, she needed to replace her coffeemaker that was lost in the move ASAP.

"Yes, ma'am," the barista said, before turning to prepare Imani's desperately needed coffee and sugar fix.

"So, if you aren't the new political science professor, then who are you?" a deep voice asked from behind her.

Imani started. Her animal and her human senses were finely tuned. No one ever snuck up on her.

No One.

She was sure there had been no one behind her or even within a fifteen-foot radius just a moment before she ordered.

Pulse racing, she turned quickly and was pleasantly surprised to see that she was staring into a chest and not a face. A broad, well-defined chest by the way that white button-down shirt was straining at the seams of his massive shoulders. He looked like he was one good bodybuilder pose away from ripping the shirt apart. Her eyes widened as she looked up and up and up before she found the midnight skin and chiseled face of a Maasi warrior staring down at her. Imani's breath caught in her throat as his onyx eyes bored into her own amber ones.

"Imani Wilson, strength and conditioning coach in the athletic department," she coughed out.

She offered her hand.

It was swallowed by his large smooth hand. "I'm Ansel Junaid, Adjunct Professor, Political Science, and it is an absolute pleasure to meet you, Ms. Wilson."

The moment their skin touched, she felt an electric spark shoot up her arm to her elbow and radiate throughout her body leaving unnerving tingles prickling her skin. All the fine hairs on her body lifted. Imani had once gotten shocked plugging a lamp with a short in the cord into a socket. This electric jolt was at minimum fifty times stronger than that jolt, and it touched every nerve on her body.

She pulled her hand back slowly.

Imani didn't want to startle whatever animal that lived in Ansel because she could feel the eyes of the animal inside him looking out through Ansel's eyes as well. The intensity of two of them staring directly into her eyes knocked the breath out of her for a moment. Her heart started racing at triple time. She felt her animal perk up with an intense curiosity she normally didn't display at meeting strangers or anyone. Imani decided not to ponder her animal's interest. Pushing both her physical reaction and her own animal's intense curiosity to the back of her mind for review later, much later.

"Nice to meet you, Professor," she answered as coolly as she could. Before Imani could say more or decide if now was an appropriate time to run from the dining hall or better yet the state, she was interrupted.

"Ma'am, one extra-large coffee with seven creams and seven sugars. That will be four dollars."

"Add it to my bill, Keisha," Ansel said just as Imani turned and held out a five-dollar bill to Keisha.

Keisha made no move to take the five-dollar bill from Imani's hand. She just stood there with the coffee cup nestled between her hands waiting. Wisely, Keisha kept looking between both like a crowd at a tennis match watching players volley. She stood patiently waiting for Imani or Ansel's directions.

Imani turned her head back in Ansel's direction slightly. He had stepped closer to her while she was turned around. She had been expecting a quick grab of her coffee off the metal counter. Then scooting away as fast as her legs could carry her from the piercing eyes of Ansel and his animal.

"Thanks, but no thanks, Professor." She turned back to face him. Something told her that being around this man was not safe. Even though she sensed no physical danger from him. She needed fresh air because he was still crowding the air in her lungs. Against her normal instincts of fight first, she needed to flee and to get away quickly.

"I'm Ansel, not Professor. Please let me buy your coffee and a muffin? I insist, for frightening you."

"You didn't frighten me, Professor," Imani lied.

Ansel's left eyebrow shot upward. She knew he had detected the lie; but was being polite enough to not call her out. He still pushed. "Maybe another time then."

"Um, sure...maybe some other time." Imani grabbed the coffee from Keisha's hand, dropped the five-dollar bill and practically race-walked away using her long legs to put as much distance between them as she could. She would spend time alone with the sexy Professor and his intense animal on the first of Neveruary.

"He sounds fah-nine!" Davida whisper squealed through her Bluetooth. "What does he look like? Please say at least half as sexy as that voice. That voice shouldn't be wasted on an ugly or short or fat dude."

Imani cleared the doorway and turned to see where Ansel was standing. Luckily for her he was still standing at the coffee kiosk on the opposite side of the room, talking animatedly to Keisha.

Imani took a moment to let her eyes linger over Ansel from the top of his perfectly rounded bald head to neatly trimmed beard and mustache, his crisply starched white shirt and tailored heather grey slacks to the bottom of his large feet clad in leather oxfords. Her slow perusal of his body was something she would have preferred to do while she was up close, and they were both undressed.

She pushed the animal's thought back to the back of her mind again. She could feel her pacing and whining. Her animal wanting to do nothing else but head right back over to the Professor and breathe in his scent.

Sighing, she turned skipping down the steep stone steps and headed toward the athletic complex sipping her coffee as she went. "He looks like an extra tall version of Djimon Hounsou before he started dating Kimora."

Davida sighed deeply, then cursed, "You have all the luck. Why aren't you still back there drinking your diabetic coffee and flirting with that man? Even I could hear the interest in his voice, and you know I'm practically immune to that sort of thing." Most lionesses had to have a male lion shifter physically jump on them to show interest because they didn't recognize flirting, Davida was even worse than most lionesses.

Imani crossed the street on the flashing white man in the box. "Because, Davida, this is my first day here and I didn't move halfway across the country to meet a man."

"Look, Imani, I know why you moved. Haven't I been here the whole time listening to you bitch and moan about how unfair your mother and grandmother are treating you? Haven't I been supportive the whole time? BUT that man sounds delicious like freshly baked chocolate cake with a ton of frosting and your aunt's caramel drizzle. On top of that I guarantee he's virile enough to get me pregnant through the phone. Don't get caught up in the new job and hiding from your family that you forget to have fun. And he sounds like he is every woman shifter's idea of fun."

The beige bricked basketball arena loomed in front of Imani. She stopped on the corner to look at the entire edifice. She took a long sip of her coffee. Pure Colombian ecstasy hit her taste buds giving her the instant sugar laced caffeine rush she needed to be clear headed. The tension started to melt from her body as she took another sip. "Girl, are you in heat?" Imani tried to remember the last time, Davida's pride went into heat, but it escaped her. She rushed on. "The last thing I need is a man distracting me from establishing myself here." Taking a third long sip of her coffee that almost drained the cup, Imani prepared to say goodbye. "I'm outside the gym. I'll call you later. Bye!"

"I'm not in heat," Davida snapped before saying, "Bye! Have a great first day. Call me after!"

The two friends disconnected, and Imani turned her phone off. She knew her family would soon begin their morning rounds of calls and didn't want her embarrassing personalized ringtones for each of her aunts to sing out across the gym. She took three deep breaths to relax herself before heading inside on her first day.

Chapter Two
The Longest Day

"I am very pleased to welcome Imani Wilson to our athletic department." Acting Athletic Director and basketball Head Coach Henry "Hook Shot" Marvin beamed at her and clapped thunderously while looking to the other coaches as they sat at the nine a.m. department meeting. "Coach Wilson, do you have a few words? Maybe you want to introduce yourself and tell us about your background?"

The other coaches' applause could be best described as lukewarm, the polite kind given to a standup comedian who bombed at an open mic.

He gestured for her to stand. Imani stood to her full six foot one-inch height and adjusted the zipper of her track suit. "I'm Imani," she paused temporarily, at a loss for words as she looked around the dingy athletic office with its faded athletic posters, scarred desks and dirty mustard smeared walls. She noticed one guy smirk at her lapse. That smirk jerked her back. "I was formerly the assistant athletic trainer at Clark Atlantic. My undergrad and master's degrees are in Kinesiology, both from Clark Atlantic University. I look forward to being here and helping the Wildcats get to the top of the Red River conference in every sport."

She sat down quickly in the armless wooden chair. Her chair squeaked alarmingly, and she felt the wood give on the left side. Using her shifter speed, she stood quickly as the chair collapsed into a broken heap behind her.

Snickers erupted around the room, and someone coughed out, "Fat ass."

Imani felt her animal rising to the surface. The animal's way was always to quash any slight— perceived or otherwise —-with violence. Sternly, she warned her animal that there could be no violence, not on her first day at a new job.

She shoved her hands in her pockets and pushed her embarrassment down. She stepped to the side as Coach Marvin and another coach rushed toward her.

"Any questions for Coach Wilson?" Henry asked as he pulled a newer chair forward for her.

"What sports did you train at Clark Atlantic?" Someone threw out, trying no doubt to get onto Coach Marvin's good side. Coach Marvin stood at the front of the room, not full on glaring but giving everyone hard stares like a mother silently scolding a toddler in the grocery store.

"Men's track and field, basketball and baseball and all women's athletics," Imani answered flatly.

"Why did you leave Clark Atlantic?"

"I came here." She kept her answers vague, not really in the mood to explain her family, Herd dynamics, or anything else to a group of strangers – especially her new mixed group of coworkers with as far as she could tell both human and shifter. She could barely get other shifters sometimes to understand the dynamics of a Herd because they hadn't been born into the Herd life.

"What kind of shifter are you?"

Everyone around the room gasped, humans and shifters alike. Asking what kind of shifter, a person was, was the height of rude. It didn't surprise Imani that it was the Smirker who asked.

"Coach Harrison, that isn't an appropriate question," Coach Marvin admonished. "I apologize, Coach Wilson."

Before she knew it, she was standing at the table in front of where the Smirker sat stunned by her quick movement across the width of the room. Her height allowed her to lean over the narrow table getting directly into the Smirker's face. "I'm the Scary kind of shifter. I'm the one your mother threatened to feed you to as a child. If you think you're scarier than me, then show me yours and I'll show you mine." She allowed just enough of her alpha powers loose to test his animal's power. She pushed her tendril of power into his face.

A little alpha challenge.

His chocolate brown eyes widened and then his upside down, spade shaped nostrils flared. His whole body jerked like he'd been struck by the full voltage of a cattle prod. Before Imani could stop him, he slid out of his chair, getting down on his hands and knees on the floor in full supplication.

Imani stood to her full height and smirked hard enough for her dimples to appear. She pulled her tendril of power back into herself. She pulled up the new chair Coach Marvin had brought for her and sat slowly before asking, "Any more questions?"

There was an awkward pause as all the coaches and assistant coaches stared at her and then at Coach Harrison still on the floor and back at her.

"That will be all for this meeting," Coach Marvin said.

The assembled coaches and the rest of the athletic staff scurried out of the room. Imani sighed. This was not the best way to start at a new job being the scary out-of-control Alpha female the staff had to flee for their lives from because she attacked a fellow employee.

"Coach Wilson, I'll show you to your office. Space is at a premium, so you'll be sharing with Coach Gleason. She isn't here this week. It is her last month of maternity leave, but she will be back in the next week or so," Coach Marvin said, leading Imani out of the room and down a hallway.

"Coach Marvin, I apologize for what happened in there," Imani said quickly as she hurried to follow Coach Marvin's long stride down the purple and gray striped corridor.

"No need, Imani, I've known your family for years and years. That bit of rudeness should not be something any shifter should have to endure much less a female alpha of a matriarchal line such as yours. And speaking of matriarchal line, how is your mother doing these days?" Coach Marvin turned with such a hopeful look in his walnut-colored eyes that Imani at once felt sorry for him.

"She's pretty busy these days running the Herd, now that my grandmother has officially retired."

Coach Marvin opened the door to a tiny office that was made even more cramped by the two large desks shoved into it. The desks faced one another with not even a half an inch of space between them. The chairs scrapped the wood paneled walls behind them. Cracked linoleum matched the rest of the floors of the gymnasium. Above, a popcorn ceiling loomed too low for Imani's comfort. One desk was covered by seven stacks of paper, an overflowing inbox, computer monitor and a Dell computer tower, half a dozen picture frames filled with happy children's faces, paperweights, candles, figurines, desk lamp and enough pencils to rebuild a tree.

The other desk had a large desk blotter with an earlier calendar year's number across the top and nothing else.

"I guess I am really starting from scratch," Imani whispered to herself.

Coach Marvin must have heard her whisper. He said sincerely, "We are extremely lucky to have you here, Imani. We've never had a full-time strength and conditioning coach. Most of the time, it is up to the coach of each team to run the training sessions or the athletes come in and train on their own. Thankfully, the Red River Conference made it mandatory so that the College released the funds."

"Thanks, Coach Marvin. It'll be an adventure to help improve all the athlete's overall fitness and watch it translate to the field or court or track and hopefully a winning record. I'll just need a few things to get started. A computer, a roster of all the student athletes, what sport or sports they play, any injuries currently, but also any injuries they've experienced in the past in case I need to modify..." she paused reached across her empty desk to the overflowing one to grab a pencil and Post-it note, but paused with her hand in midair, not wanting to mark her scent across her new colleague's desk to let her know that someone had been there if she was a shifter.

"Coach Marvin, is Coach Gleason a...?"

"No, no, she's a regular human," Coach Marvin explained. "She's married to a first-generation Carrier. There's a rumor that they may have finally had a Shifter child this time." Waving to the six picture frames, he left unsaid the genetic improbability of a human and a first-generation Carrier having a full shifter child. Coach Marvin backed out of the office because there wasn't much room to turn around unless he about-faced military style. "Let me show you where the supplies are kept."

She followed him down another dimly lit corridor to the left. He opened another unmarked door with a thick set of keys he pulled from his pocket. This door opened to a walk-in closet filled to the brink with every conceivable office supply including a new convertible ultrabook computer still in the box.

"I bought that after you came out for the interview. I saw the one you were using and thought it would be great to get each of the whole staff one, but the budget wouldn't allow for it now. New desktop computers were purchased three years ago, so new computers won't be bought for at least another year or two or even three years, if not longer. I plan to replace all those desktops when they break down with ultrabooks or laptops." Waving a hand at the supplies. "Take anything else you need. Just lock the door behind you. Last week, I put in a ticket with the Help Desk for someone to get your email set up, but of course stuff like that is," he made air quotes with his fingers, 'low priority', but hopefully someone from the Not So Helpful Desk will be by your office today."

Imani quickly grabbed a box of pens, a few packs of different colored and sized sticky notes, a couple of notebooks, and the convertible ultrabook. "This be enough to get me started. Thanks, Coach Marvin."

"Please, call me Henry or Coach Henry if you prefer. You know, your mother and I were matched for a very short time by your grandmother and my mother. Of course, that was before the Peace and your father was given to your mother as part of the treaty."

"Oh really?" Imani feigned innocence, trying and failing for a sweet and innocent expression.

She knew all the details of her mother's and Coach Henry's

proposed marriage, the unfinished marriage contract that her grandmother and his mother negotiated, and their entire fourteen-day long engagement, which, was just long enough for him to develop an unrequited crush that was still alive and kicking thirty years later. Luckily for Coach Henry, her father had passed away over a decade ago. Unluckily for him, Imani's mom and dad may have had a quick, politically arranged marriage, but they fell deeply in love. Imani's mother, Josephine, hadn't looked twice at another shifter or human or magic wielder in the past decade since his death. She tries to convince everyone that she will remain a widow for life.

"Yes, your mother was the most beautiful woman I had ever seen up until I was matched with my late wife, Annabelle."

"Our Herd was saddened to hear of your Herd's loss," Imani said diplomatically. Coach Henry's wife had passed away over a year ago.

Henry's wife, Annabelle, was the Beta of their Herd. Their marriage was a complicated political maneuver and was arranged in the same treaty in which Imani's own parents were matched. The pairing was a complete step down from her mother's Alpha rank, but he seemed to have been happy. He even got to remain with his own family Herd, which made him the most powerful male in his Herd. Most bull elephants joined their wife's family Herd at marriage.

"I came in early and observed the soccer team's practice this morning," she said by way of distraction. "I watched all of last year's soccer matches that were available online. Many of your players especially on the men's team, started suffering from fatigue in the last twelve to fifteen minutes of the match. Your coach tried to disguise it with a lot of substitutions. The team has a couple of standout athletes who could play anywhere in the world, but they need more tools to get them ready for the pro or semi-pro level. Soccer isn't really a game, it's a ninety-minute endurance test while kicking a ball. I'm going to draft a couple of versions of new training schedules to help them build more endurance. It will be a couple of weeks before the results translate to the field, but the results will be evident in the win column."

"Well, Imani, I don't think you will have any trouble getting Coach Harrison to follow any new routine you want to establish. I'll go check the conference room to see if he has gotten off the floor and send him your way after lunch." He chuckled. "Will that work?"

"Thanks, Coach Henry."

Imani turned with her supplies and headed back to her office. She sat gingerly in her brown leather desk chair. It held her weight without a groan, and the leather was supple. Settling in, she opened one of the Black and Red notebooks she had grabbed and finished the list she had begun composing for Coach Henry earlier.

Quietly, she seethed that the coach she would need to work with first would be the men's soccer coach who her animal had to confront before she'd even learned his name. Dropping her pen, Imani closed her eyes, concentrating on working her way through a series of deep breathing exercises one of her aunts had taught her to calm down the raging beast she carried inside of her. She imagined the excess emotions dissipating out through her nose, breathing calm in and anger out. After several minutes, she felt her emotional equilibrium click to more acceptable levels. Her emotions weren't balanced, but that would be impossible to achieve without shifting.

She worked quietly and quickly for the better part of two hours, composing lists and designing a training program for all sports in season, the men's and women's soccer team, and then the cross-country team. Basketball and the other sports would have to wait for now since they weren't in season.

At eleven thirty a.m., her stomach loudly announced it was lunch time. Imani reached into her pocket and turned her cell on as she stood to make her way to the dining hall. Back in Atlanta, she normally brought a lunch that one of her aunts packed for her or went home for lunch to the Herd House.

She made her way back across the small suburban campus to the only dining hall, already missing lunches from her aunts and with her family.

Chapter Three
Calls of The Herd

As soon as her cell phone hit a cell tower, it began ringing. Aunt Joyce's fake mean mug appeared on her screen. "Hello, Aunt Joyce."

"Hey, Lovebutton! How is the first day going?"

"It's going pretty good, Auntie," Imani fibbed. The less her aunts worried, the better.

Aunt Joyce quipped in her languid Georgia drawl, "Is that Henry Heartbreaker trying to get you to give him your mother's personal cell number yet? It was the best day of his life the day Mother matched your mother and him together. I swear up and down he almost drooled on himself the first time he met your mother. She was wearing an emerald green dress. You know how good she looks in green, right? She looks good in any shade of green really, but emerald just sets her apart. Well, I remember this dress especially because mother had a bunch of dresses, like a dozen or so made up by the seamstress, and she brought them home one day. They were all the same pattern, mostly different sizes and fabrics. All of us girls were fighting over the dresses and Mother was like 'if you don't try those on and see what fits who best – I'll give them all to the Salvation Army. You know how scary Mother can be when she yells; I guess raising a bunch of teenage girls can turn you into a monster, but Dad is still even-keeled, but Anyhoo. So of course, we tried them on and that one fit your mother the best. Even though me and Jasmine wanted it." Aunt Joyce spoke in paragraphs, and it was best to just let her talk herself out.

The problem was that her Georgia accent was like waiting for cold honey to drip from a bottle. Everyone called her Aunt Chatterbox, but not to her face. Butting into her mostly one-sided conversation just wasn't heard by Aunt Chatterbox at all, and the listener just had to keep on listening, then pounce once she slowed for a breath.

Imani slipped her Bluetooth back in her ear and kept walking. She punctuated every seventh sentence with an "uh huh," "oh no," or "okay."

Twenty minutes later, Imani had finished her large chef's salad. She hated eating salads and combatted her hatred by drowning every salad with as much salad dressing as possible. Her stopping point was just shy of it becoming a soupy mess. Aunt Joyce was still in full stream of conscious and she didn't sound like she was going to slow down in the least. Imani took a brisk jog around the seven blocks of campus, trying to burn some of her excess energy off. During her lunch breaks at Clark Atlantic, she would meet with some other ladies who belonged to the non-profit group, Black Girls Run. They would run five kilometers three days a week. Her last day running with the group had been more of a tear-filled walk in which they had tried to talk her into staying like the rest of her family.

Most of them were human, they had no understanding of the pressures that she was under from the Herd. She couldn't tell them that her mother and grandmother had unceremoniously presented her with a list of twenty-five, newly approved, pre-screened names of male shifters that had been vetted by the Herd's matchmaker. Every criteria of a possible pairing had been considered from their nuclear family, extended family connections, current personal wealth and even projections of wealth, future political ambitions – in both Shifter Society and the world at large and most important genetics.

After she was to have reviewed all of their dossiers, the Herd had arranged a formal meet and greet where she was to make her top three selections. Once her top three selections agreed to the match, the Herd would enter into formal marriage contract negotiations. Whoever was the final shifter standing would then propose at a fancy engagement party filled with the Herd, friends and with the crème de la crème of Atlanta's shifter society to bear witness. Then have a long, but not too long engagement, but still marry as quickly as the wedding could be planned and not smack of desperation. Finally, start having babies within the first year of marriage. Lots of babies. Hopefully, girl babies and hopefully one every year for the next decade or even longer.

If shifter babies could be guaranteed through IVF or other fertility treatments, then she was sure her Herd would have started pressuring her to take that route regardless of if she found a proper shifter male or not. Her thoughts of elephant mating practices had chased her to the furthest end of campus. The invisible line that separated the residential homes from the campus 'proper.' Imani turned around and went back to her office. She barely remembered Aunt Joyce was on the phone carrying on her one-sided conversation filling her ear with all the gossip of home.

"Hey, Aunt Joyce," Imani said four times before Aunt Joyce heard her over her own half of the conversation. "My lunch break is over, and I'm back at the office."

"Okay, dear, call me if you're' feeling homesick later. Pete and I are going to try those salsa lessons at the community center, but you know I have two left human feet so anything to get me out of dancing would be greatly appreciated."

Imani laughed. "Just talking to you now has made me feel better. Thanks for calling, Aunt Joyce."

"You're welcome, Lovebutton!" Imani disconnected the call.

Imani walked back into her office and sighed. Just walking into the office felt like she was going spelunking into a cave system. Her office at Clark Atlantic had floor to ceiling windows with bright sunshine streaming in and was twice the size of this one. Even though here at Wiley, she was only sharing with one person. She pulled out a stack of Post-it notes and booted up the computer for the first time. As Henry had indicated, nothing was set up. She let it begin to run one hundred and two updates and took out her phone, going to the Pinterest app to look for office decorating tips. Forty-five minutes later she had filled three, large sticky notes full of ideas to decorate her side of the office. Two other notes held ideas for her and her new office mate, Coach Gleason, to discuss for the entire space. Sometime next week she would also ask Coach Henry if she could pry the seventies wood paneling off the wall. Even if she had to snatch it off with her bare hands.

She spent another twenty minutes Googling home decor stores and their directions. Tonight, she would spend time shopping to decorate her new apartment and her office, and she wouldn't need to call Aunt Joyce or anyone else because she was homesick.

Just as she was Googling the Marshall, Texas, public library, her phone rang again playing *"The Devil Went Down to Georgia."*

Imani sighed. Leave it to Aunt Joyce to spread the word that her phone was on. Aunt Joanne's smiling face appeared across her screen as she was about to hit the magnifying glass.

"Hi, Aunt Joanne."

"Look, if you don't like it, I can have the nephews there tomorrow to pack you up and bring you home where you belong," Aunt Joanne begin without preamble.

Imani had long ago concluded that if her mother wasn't the Alpha of her generation that Aunt Joanne would have gladly stepped into the breach. Josephine may run the entire Herd, but Aunt Joanne had charge of the bulls and young males and let her tell it to all the males.

"Aunt Joanne, I'm fine. I promise."

"Then why was your phone off this morning, huh?" she inquired like Detective Stabler from her favorite Law & Order franchise.

She could picture her aunt trying to bore into her eyes with a slight sideways tilt to her head with Stabler's trademark disbelief and fury. Imani smiled at the image.

"There were meetings this morning." Imani leaned as far back in her chair as the wall would allow and stared at the disgusting stained popcorn ceiling while Aunt Joanne launched into her tirade. Imani scented a presence, moments before a timid knock on the door frame. "E-mani Wilson?"

"I'm Imani."

"Derrick Jackson from IT Helpdesk. I have a service ticket to set up your computer."

"Aunt Joanne, I have..."

"I heard. Look Niece, the minute you feel uncomfortable or overwhelmed you call, and I'll send the nephews out on the next flight. You'll be packed up and back in the Herd House before the end of the day!"

"Yes, Aunt." Imani sighed. She saw 'call ended' on her screen and quickly powered her phone down before another Aunt called. She stood quickly and moved out of the way so that Derrick could access the computer.

"Quite a few updates here, I see. I can't get to work until they finish."

"I understand." Imani moved to the other side of the office and sat in Coach Gleason's chair. She regretted the decision as soon as she heard the chair groan. She stood once again, not trusting any chair besides her own at this point.

Those chairs were going to give her a complex. Yes, at a size eighteen, she was considered plus size by human standards, but she was an elephant shifter; she had to carry a certain amount of body weight. There was no effortless way to pack fourteen thousand pounds into a human body even with the innate magic of a shifter body.

Derrick said absolutely nothing, and she decided to follow his lead. The silence stretched out between them as the minutes grew from one to forty as they waited for the ultrabook to update. The sound of a rebooting computer was the best sound that Imani had heard all day. Derrick pounced on the computer, furiously typing as he set up her computer.

"I built your profile a couple of days ago. I double-checked it before coming over, so all I really need to do is connect you to the server." He pulled out a piece of paper that resembled a bad origami experiment. "This is your email and temporary password. You'll need to change your password." He placed the paper next to the computer. He stood and left without another word.

"Well, buh bye then," Imani said to the empty door. She shook her head but sat down in her own chair gratefully. She couldn't decide if the IT guy's response was because most IT guys were weird or if he had heard about her interaction with Coach Harrison this morning. Embarrassment burned away at the bottom of her throat like heartburn.

Opening her Outlook, there were thirty messages waiting for her. Twelve were from Coach Henry with rosters and schedules and one just thanking her for joining his athletic department, which seemed just a little premature since he was only the acting athletic director, but he had an inside scoop.

Coach Harrison appeared in the door. She knew he had decided to come and apologize to her. Small motes of her Alpha power clung to him, and she could have tracked him magically across the state and all parts of the country if she wanted. Unfortunately, he had waited fifty-seven minutes before appearing before her. The animal in her was a vengeful beast who was not going to offer him any mercy. The elephant inside of her couldn't allow herself to be disrespected by a male and especially one who wasn't an Alpha. It wasn't the matriarch way.

"Coach Imani."

"I didn't give you leave to use my first name," Imani snapped. She knew her eyes had darkened and looked like glowing amber orbs from some horror movie director's imagination. Her animal was still smarting from being challenged, and she was definitely angry at being called a fat ass.

"I apologize, Coach Wilson. I came to offer my sincerest apologies to you for being so rude and disrespectful this morning."

"You have to know better. I can't believe that either your Alpha or your mother would sanction the conduct you displayed this morning. I will need their full names, addresses and numbers so that I can speak with them and report your behavior."

When dark skinned men paled, they went ashen, and Coach Harrison looked like he had run headlong through a falling bag of flour. "That isn't necessary."

"I disagree. If one of the people under my command ever behaved in such a manner, I would need to know. Need. To. Know," she emphasized.

"Coach Wilson, I beg you…"

"Do I need to go to Coach Marvin for this information?" She slid a notebook and pen to the edge of the desk opened to a blank page. "I'm new to the shifter community here in Texas, but we Georgians don't allow for that amount of disrespect to another shifter, much less an Alpha. Is it because you didn't know I was an Alpha that you decided to disrespect me?"

"I… I—"

"Is it because I'm a woman that you disrespected me?"

"I… I—"

"If I wouldn't tear this room and this part of the building to shreds, I would shift right now and teach you the manners you failed to use this morning. Have you ever been gored, Coach Harrison?" She narrowed her eyes and let her angry animal rise to the surface. She could feel the fear roll off Harrison in waves as more and more of her powers unfurled.

She could smell the fear leaking off the coach in an ammonia-tinged funk. Mentally she added purchase cleaning supplies and candles to her to-do list. The smell of fear was the worst to wash out.

"I am an ALPHA. Capital A. Capital. L. Capital P. Capital H. Capital A. You will treat me with the same respect that you treat the Alpha of your…" she paused to take a huge sniff of Coach Harrison, "wolf pack. Are we understood?"

Coach Harrison came the three steps forward and with a shaking hand wrote both his mother's and Alpha's name, addresses, and phone numbers.

"When is the best time to contact them?"

He sighed so dramatically; Imani felt like he was one of the teen bulls in her Herd. "You can catch them tonight at the Chapter House. There is a meeting at eight tonight; they both will be there."

Imani pushed the notebook closer to Coach Harrison again. "I'll need that address, too."

Coach Harrison reluctantly provided her the requested info, writing neatly in small block letters in her notebook.

"Thank you. Now back to work-related issues. I came in early to observe this morning's practice, as well as most of last season's videos that I could find online. I understand that you weren't the Head Coach then, but a lot of your players" endurance levels flagged at the end of the game."

She gestured for him to speak.

He just nodded, acknowledging her observations but adding nothing else.

Imani continued, "I've created a couple of new training programs for the soccer team to boost their endurance as well as increase their overall fitness levels. I'll email you the plans, and we can begin whenever you like, I suggest as soon as possible at tomorrow's practice or this afternoon."

"Whenever you like is fine with me, Coach Wilson," he began.

Imani cut him off before all their interactions became him deferring to her. She pulled her powers back in tightly. On the outside now, she appeared just as powerless as any human. She was going to have a grim time washing his fear smell out; she didn't want to add more cleaning to her list because she let the beast's temper flare.

"Your team, your choice. Read over the training schedules before you decide and email me which one you prefer. I'll be here until five. I can also be here for the six a.m. practice session tomorrow to begin the new training regime with the players directly, if you like."

Before either of them could continue, Coach Marvin appeared in the doorway, looking alarmed. "Imani, is something wrong?" Coach Henry, as the only other elephant shifter nearby, must have felt the full fury of her powers though the walls and been the only shifter brave enough to come see what the problem was that caused the raging whitewater current of Alpha anger in the atmosphere.

"Everything is fine, Coach Henry." Imani smiled, showing both of her half inch deep dimples to show no hard feelings were taking place. "I did have a couple of questions of a personal nature if I could borrow you for an afternoon snack. I saw a sign that the coffee kiosk sells fresh baked cookies in the afternoon. I'll treat."

Coach Henry laughed weakly, still looking between Imani and Coach Harrison to gauge the temperature of the room. "Those cookies are barely passable as cookies. I think they use a frozen dough, but my sister runs a bakery a few minutes' drive from here. I can guarantee the best fresh baked brownie you have ever had. I'll meet you out front in ten minutes?"

"Brownies are my weakness. I'll be outside in five minutes." Imani stood, wanting to run to the ladies' room before she left.

Coach Henry backed his six-foot seven-inch frame out of the office again.

"Coach Harrison, is there something else?"

"No... I'll look at that email and let you know," he said staring down at his shoes.

"I look forward to your email. If you'll excuse me." Imani left, hurrying to the dusty ladies' room she had spotted earlier. She double checked her pockets for her wallet and cell phone as she went.

Seven minutes later she was standing in front of the arena. She noticed even more wear and tear to the building that she hadn't paid any attention to during her initial visit. The whole edifice looked and felt worn and dingy. Had she been so desperate to get away from her family that she just ignored the obvious signs of substandard maintenance and an athletic program teetering on the brink of financial hardship?

Obviously.

She was here now with only herself to blame for the rush to get away. Maybe she should have listened to Davida's astute counseling and tried to negotiate with her mother or her grandmother or even tried to appeal directly to the Herd instead of accepting a new position, some nine and a half hours away from home. She could feel the pit in her chest expand as she launched into another round of regretting her hasty decisions for the umpteenth time since she left Atlanta Saturday morning.

She turned her cell on and wasn't surprised that it promptly started playing Ace of Base's *"I Saw the Sign"* her ringtone for her almost, but not quite truly psychic Aunt Jasmine.

"Hi, Aunt Jasmine."

"You meet a man today."

"I did start a new job today, so I met several new people some even being of the male persuasion,". Imani said drolly. There was nothing her Aunt Jasmine hated more than sarcasm, which is why Imani had become fluent in it as a toddler following her aunt around the bakery. Her chest pain lightened just getting to mess with her favorite aunt.

"Don't get sassy mouthed with me, young lady. I will filet you and bake you into a pie and feed you to your mother. You know exactly the man I'm talking about. Tall, very handsome, he scared you?" Aunt Jasmine swung between being *Professor Trelawney* and *Bellatrix Lestrange* within the space of the same heartbeat. The whole family just let sleeping psychics lie.

"Yes, Auntie. I know the one you are talking about," Imani answered, briefly chastised. Her aunt in a towering rampage was indeed vindictive enough to carve Imani up into bite sized pieces.

"Keep away from him. He is in danger."

"I didn't move halfway across the country to meet a man, Auntie. I have no intention of even having coffee with him, much less hooking up, Netflix and chilling, sliding into his DM's or anything else with him."

"His kind don't hook up or whatever else you just said." Imani pictured her aunt's long, slender brown fingers covered in some type of bread dough making air quotes around the phrase 'hook up'. "And he is at a critical state in choosing a mate and we don't want you considered as a contender. Make sure you do your best to stay out of his path. Tell Henrietta I said, 'hello and that I still make the best brownies.' Don't buy that red rug it will shed dreadfully, get the bronze one instead. Toodles," Jasmine said in a rush before hanging up.

Imani looked at her phone and Jasmine had ended the call in under five minutes. Exactly four minutes and fifty-nine seconds. All her calls were under five minutes, never longer. It was a running joke in the family that if a Jasmine call went over five minutes, you were going to die.

Coach Henry came striding out of the arena, keys in hand and looking very aggravated. His stride was heavy. The telltale double stomp, stomp of an elephant shifter ready to rampage. She followed him wordlessly to his new jacked up, cherry red Ford F-150 with paper tags still on it. He unlocked the passenger side door for her and waited for her to get in before walking around and hopping in the driver's side. Moments later they rolled out of the lot and headed away from campus.

Henry drove in silence, strumming his fingers on the steering wheel. The radio was off. "Coach Henry, I was wondering if you could introduce me to the local Alpha so that they can introduce me at the local Council or at least tell me where I can find them. I need to present myself."

"I'll ask my sister," he said quietly.

In elephant shifters, females ran the Herd period. Just like a herd in the wild, they handed out the discipline, assigned the duties, managed the bloodlines and genetics, arranged marriages, and even declared war. Imani was in another Herd's territory and even though it was now permitted under the Treaty of the Great Shifter War, she felt it would be ill mannered not to introduce herself officially to the local Herd and the other Alphas.

"I'd appreciate that."

Henry had lapsed back into silence and she joined him. Imani watched as the streets grew wider, the homes grew larger and the businesses were more prosperous. She hadn't been on this side of town and regretted renting her apartment sight unseen from a Craigslist ad and over the phone from Atlanta.

She would send her lease to Aunt Jackie and see if she could break it. She had opted for the shortest lease the landlord offered, but three days in and she was ready to go. These apartments were larger, modern and looked more diverse. Just before Imani felt compelled to pick up the conversation that was dropped, Coach Henry turned into a shopping center. He parked in front of the Patty Cake Bakery with a large powder blue and white stripped awning covering the front of the shop. The storefront looked simple and old fashioned, but modern at the same time with its large white planters filled with flowers and electronic board flashing specials.

"This is my sister's place. Ready for the best brownie you've ever had?" Whatever had been bothering Henry, he was now making a conscious effort to hide his upset.

"I'll try anything chocolate. Lead the way." They reached for door handles at the same time.

"Welcome to the Patty Cake Bakery," a cheerful voice called from the back as the two walked into the cool, brightly lit store. "I'll be right out."

Imani inhaled deeply. This bakery was all desserts and smelled primarily of chocolate, brown sugar and vanilla extract. Aunt Jasmine's place smelled of several types of flours, yeast and warm bread. Her stomach whimpered.

"It's me!" Henry gave a little shout.

"Oh, well then, I won't rush at all," she called back.

Imani walked to the glass display case. Cookies of all shapes and sizes by the dozen, mini cakes, large cakes with mirror glazed frosting, mini pies, large pies with towering meringues, fruit tarts, brownies, blondies and desserts that Imani had no names for were packed into the twenty foot long display case as far as the eye could see. Her eyes danced over all the offerings. She had walked into the Willie Wonka of bakeries.

"Everything looks amazing." Imani sighed. She mentally started tallying her caloric intake for the day because she was about to blow it out for the rest of the month. She pulled out her wallet, getting two, fresh new twenty-dollar bills. Coach Henry placed his large hand over her hands and wallet.

"Your money is no good here."

"But I plan on getting several things."

"My sister is not going to allow you to pay your first visit."

"That's right, but next time I'll charge you double," a statuesque woman with skin the color of pure honey declared from the other side of the counter. Her wide set eyes traveled the length and width of Imani in mere seconds. "Who is this lovely child here, Henry?"

"This is Imani Wilson. My new strength and conditioning coach. She's Josephine Trudeau's daughter. Imani, this is my sister Henrietta Marvin, she is the Alpha here."

"Well in that case I'll just charge you regular price. You look like your mother especially around the eyes." Her own eyes crinkled in the corners as she smiled at Imani.

Before thoughts of her mother could drag her down, Imani switched topics. "My Aunt Jasmine wanted me to say 'Hello' and to tell you that she still bakes the best brownies."

"That old mind reading witch! You tell her I still haven't forgiven her leaving me with the Worst Roommate In The World when we were in culinary school together," Henrietta said smiling while giving Imani a second, more thorough going over.

Imani hated when she met other Alpha females especially Alpha werelephants. Most of them were like her mother a little hardnosed and a lot of judgmental. Imani was a super plus size and extra weight was considered a no-no even over her six-foot one-inch frame.

Henrietta came around the counter of display cases. "Give me a hug, child. You look like you could use one." Henrietta enveloped Imani is a tight hug.

She held on to Henrietta inhaling the scent of brown sugar and vanilla as Henrietta leaned into the hug and let her healing powers rush over them.

What felt like an hour passed as they stood in the embrace, but it was only a couple of moments. "Things not going as you wanted?" Henrietta whispered.

Imani could only nod.

"It's okay, not everything starts off as smooth as we want.

I'll walk with you until you find the right path."

At that soft promise, Imani begin crying. Weeping softly, Imani pulled away from Henrietta to find a tissue.

Henry passed her an embroidered handkerchief. She wiped her eyes gently trying not to smudge her eye makeup. After a moment, she just gave up and wiped it all away.

"Thanks, Coach Henry."

"No problem, sugar. You keep that in case you need it again."

"There will be no more crying," Henrietta said coming back a few moments later. She came around the counter again with a tray which held three tall glasses of milk, three types of cookies, three types of brownies and three types of cupcakes. "I call this the 'drown your sorrows' special. No one leaves here feeling bad as long as I have cocoa."

She set the tray on one of the small cafe tables that were arranged around the shop. Imani hadn't even noticed the powder blue wrought iron cafe tables until the siblings gathered around them. White lazy Susan's sat in the center of the tables holding dessert plates, napkins and silverware. The matching wrought iron chairs were a darker powder blue and had powder blue and white striped cushions.

"Everyone else calls it Hennie's diabetic coma," Coach Henry said with a smile. He piled a brownie, three cookies and a cupcake with deep pink icing onto his plate. He walked across the bakery, sitting his plate and milk down then reached behind the wall mounted television for the remote that was velcroed to the back and turned to ESPN. He even turned the tv up loudly giving Imani and Henrietta a semblance of privacy.

Henrietta waved Imani into one of the wrought iron chairs with a powder blue and white striped cushion. She handed Imani a plate and begin her own selections from the tray. Imani chose two chocolate chip cookies, two double chocolate chip cookies, one that looked like it had cranberries, a cake brownie and a cupcake with bright yellow frosting.

Her first bite was of the cake brownie and it nearly brought her to tears again. It was so moist and airy and had just the right amounts of chocolate and even a nutty taste.

"This is the best brownie I've ever had." Stuffing a second and third bite into her mouth in quick succession followed by a long swallow of ice-cold milk.

"Make sure you tell your Aunt Jasmine THAT!" Henrietta said laughing, slapping the table.

Imani took two more bites and a swallow of milk.

"Tell me what's wrong," Henrietta asked softly.

"I'm twenty-seven and the first-born female. The next female born is twenty-two and the one after is twelve," Imani stated slowly.

Comprehension dawned immediately across Henrietta's face. "How many girls are in your generation?"

"Five."

"How many boys?"

"Sixteen."

Henrietta whistled low and long. She sat all the way back in her chair and glanced up to the ceiling with a frown. "That isn't normal at all. I can only imagine the pressure being placed on you to mate and start having children. Girl children and lots of them."

"It wasn't anything overt at first, but they started moving up my Alpha training schedule. Things that had been mapped out for the next decade were compressed down into five years. Then it was the formal dinner parties being thrown with eligible males from all over the country and various parts of the world invited. Before, when an eligible bull showed up with 'courting on his Herd's mind' as my grandmother called it; we would be polite but send them on their way. Suddenly The Herd were having formal gatherings for almost any bull or Alpha who passed the Herd's eligibility standards." She paused stuffing a double chocolate chip cookie in her mouth finishing it in two chews, then draining the last of her milk. Henrietta passed her untouched one and she drained that one too.

"After I said 'no' to all the dinner parties, it was random meetings at Starbucks or while out shopping and once even at the dentist.

These weren't just Atlanta based shifters they were trying to sneak up on me, one guy was flown out from Ohio!" She stuffed a chocolate chip cookie in her mouth. She chewed slower this time. "Mother asked me to come home for lunch one day. Melba De Vane was waiting for me at the kitchen table with pimento cheese sandwiches and lemonade."

"Melba De Vane, the television matchmaker?" Henrietta asked, instantly starstruck. "In your kitchen?"

Nodding Imani continued, "I knew I had to do something quick. So, I started applying for jobs anywhere and everywhere that was at least 500 miles from Atlanta. This was the first offer. I even took a pay cut to come here. Nothing has been right, and I've only been here three days and I'm a little panicked about all the changes." She stuffed a cookie in her mouth. She slowed down chewing considering the macadamia nuts and raspberries and the fact that she didn't have a new dentist yet.

"When my mother began the bachelor bull parade, I was barely twenty. At least your mother waited until you were an adult, but I understand. Being the Alpha Heir in a Herd, comes with crippling expectations of perfection from the Alpha herself all the way down to the youngest calf. You are a modern girl with a career, and I understand you don't want to be rushed into picking a mate and become the Herd Broodmare. There is more to that little crying jag than just the herd pressure."

"I miss my mom. I miss home. I hate my apartment. No offense to Wiley, but everything feels old and dingy and worn. Like no one takes care of it or cares that it isn't being taken care of, I'm not used to such neglect. My office has wood paneling for crying aloud. Then this morning, in the office, some low level submissive challenged me in the staff meeting in front of everyone."

"All of that is fixable except your homesickness and that takes time and new friends and adventures. Listen Wiley is old, but it will grow on you. Is today your first day?"

"Yes."

"Your first day at a new job, in a new city, away from all of your family. You are bound to get overwhelmed. Have you ever lived outside of Georgia?"

Imani shook her head no. "I've never lived outside of the Herd House," she admitted. Blinking rapidly, she tried to stop the unshed tears from coming again. She stuffed the last cookie in her mouth and concentrated on chewing.

"One of my nieces is a real estate agent, I'll have her call you and we will find you a new apartment. I'll speak to Henry about that shifter..."

"No need for that. I pushed a puff of power in his face and he got down on hands and knees in full supplication in front of the whole coaching staff. Then later when he came to apologize, I made him give me his mother's and Alpha's names and numbers."

Henrietta burst into laughter that sounded strangely like high clear church bells tolling. "Who is his Alpha?"

"I didn't even look at the name. He said there was a chapter meeting tonight at eight."

"Probably a werewolf. Wolf shifters meet the first Monday of the month. Are you going to go?"

"I don't know. I had planned to hit a couple of stores to buy some new things for my apartment." She stuffed a whole cookie in her mouth. It was another raspberry cheesecake with dried and fresh raspberries and was still warm and chewy and heart stopping good. She chewed this one the slowest of them all.

"That sounds like fun."

Nearby, a church bell tolled four times. Henry jerked at the sound. He stood rushing toward the door. He swallowed the last third of his glass of milk before dropping it and his empty plate into a bin over the trash can.

"I have a meeting with the Dean. Thanks for the sweets, Sis." Henry hugged the now standing Henrietta.

"Anytime. We'll talk about what you needed to discuss later. Call me when your meeting is over."

"It was nice to meet you, Imani. I hope you will come back soon." Henrietta grabbed a cloth napkin wrapping the last cookies and brownies from her big tray in it before pressing the whole bundle into Imani's hands.

"Actually, Henry will bring you back tomorrow and we will have more of a chance to talk."

Henry held the door open and Imani dashed thorough. They were in the jacked up red truck, on their way back to campus when Imani apologized, "I'm sorry I monopolized your sister."

"No need to apologize, besides baking, hearing people's problems is what she does best. She gets tired of all of us, so a new person was just the thing she needed." Henry smiled, reaching over to pat her hand still holding the cloth wrapped bundle of sweets.

Changing the subject, she asked shyly, "What is your meeting with the Dean about? Are you going to become the new Athletic Director?"

Henry sighed hard, like a teenager who was just told to do a chore over. "I had hopes, but it seems that the administration has started interviewing again. At this point, I don't think so."

He pulled into campus and into his reserved spot. "I'll see you later. Let me know if you need anything."

"Thanks Coach, for everything. I'll see you tomorrow." Imani waved as Coach turned and hurried toward the administration building across the street.

Imani went back inside to her office. She spent the next hour working on a conditioning plan for the women's basketball team. She also took ten minutes to marry her little pile of sticky notes into one major to do list. Another wave of homesickness washed over her as the prospect of a night alone with no one to talk.

At five p.m. she logged off her computer and turned on her cell phone. It didn't surprise her one bit that the ringtone *"Never Scarred"* by Bonecrusher started blaring.

"Hello, Aunt Jackie." She leaned back in her comfortable chair and sighed.

"Your mother has been worried all day about you. The least you could have done is call."

"I had planned to call around eight, after she had dinner. I didn't want to disturb her day," Imani reasoned. Aunt Jackie was the largest elephant in the Herd next to Imani and her grandmother. She served as the Enforcer for Herd and often on non-Herd business as well. It was best to always stay on her good side.

"Uh huh. Every time I turned toward the office today, I saw her pacing around the desk like she does when agitated." Aunt Jackie sighed. "I know she acted nonchalant when you told her you were moving, but she is upset and scared. You are the Herd Heir and living too many states away to get there in an emergency."

The Herd office is headquartered in a strip mall with several other Herd owned businesses like Uncle Pete's dry-cleaning business, a fast food burger franchise co-owned by several family members, Aunt Jasmine's bakery, a quick oil change run by Uncle Matthew and Aunt Jackie's CrossFit Box and several non-Herd owned businesses.

"She shouldn't have started with the bull parade then."

"Who taught you 'bull parade'? That is so old school!" Aunt Jackie hollered laughing. Even through her cell phone, Imani felt the reverberations of Aunt Jackie's laughter. A smile curled up the corners of her mouth before she could stop them. Jackie's booming laugh was a comfort because her serious tone often left people who didn't know her afraid and with a racing heartbeat. "That phrase was ancient when your grandmother was young."

"It doesn't matter, but it's what y'all were doing parading men in front of me until I took an interest in one. I felt a whole new set of pressures that overwhelmed me. Like your only expectation was for me to get pregnant and keep getting me pregnant; not in seeing if I would be happy."

"I know, Niecy, but we don't have enough girls to run the Herd as is right now and it has your mother overreacting. What am I talking about? It has all of us overreacting." Jackie sighed.

"I know you know this but look at it from her side; she and I and the other sisters are too old to try and push out more babies. You are young, hopefully very fertile and the future Alpha of this Herd. It made the most sense to try and get you settled."

"I know all that, but I'm not ready for all of that," Imani whispered guiltily. She knew why the Herd was pressuring her to marry and start having babies. Just the thought of marrying someone because the Herd picked them was too overwhelming for her to bear.

"You've made that perfectly clear. Please call your mother. She feels guilty and she is worried that she pushed you too far and you will never come back to the Herd and her."

"I'll call her later like I planned," Imani repeated, she ended the call, feeling hollow inside and the panic rising again. She stood and walked out of the gymnasium and walked the twelve blocks to her apartment in someone's attic.

She took the outside stairs two at a time and let herself into her miniscule apartment. She showered slowly enjoying the smell of her ginger lime body wash as it meshed with her own natural scent. Dressing in something other than athletic wear, a simple skirt and a v-neck cotton pullover in shades of green. She slid her feet into a pair of flats. Reaching back into her track suit she pulled out her to do list, transferring it, her wallet and her keys back to her purse. Just as she was reaching for her cell to toss into her purse it rang.

It was officially The Day of Aunts as Aunt Janet's stern, sphinx like expression appeared on the screen. She debated sending the call to voicemail but knew that her aunt was the type of person to just hang up and call back and call back and call back until she said exactly what she wanted to who she wanted. If there was no back down and retreat in Imani, then there was definitely none in the Beta of their Herd, Aunt Janet. Reluctantly, she swiped to answer before it went to voicemail.

"Hello?"

"One question. Should I mark you as a rogue?"

Imani stood flummoxed. Her breathing narrowed. "Are you kicking me out of the Herd?"

"No. I'm not but you did just move halfway across the country for no reason. Basically, you've abandoned your Alpha training and your duties. It seems to me that you are kicking yourself out of the Herd and most likely the family too."

Aunt Janet paused like she could hear Imani's heartbeat thundering through the phone. Her previously brightly lit apartment was dim now. She felt plunged into darkness. Once glance out of the window told her that the sun was still up in the sky. It was her own world that was crashing around her. Janet's question was an overpowering shadow eclipsing her thoughts.

"I'm not a rogue, Aunt Janet." The words came out on a whisper. She couldn't pull in a full lungful of air. She tried again to take a deep breath, but the air in her apartment felt superheated to volcanic temperatures. It burned going into her lungs, it constricted her whole chest like a vise.

"I just want to make it official. Are you Herd or not?" Janet asked. Her persistence pushed into Imani's eardrum loudly and clearly, ramming into her brain with the impact of a jackhammer.

Was she willing to give up her family? Her future Herd? Her mother? Her grandparents? Her Aunts? Imani being declared rogue meant she would repudiate her bloodline, her inheritance and everything elephant. Everything Herd would be off limits to her for the rest of her life. She would be alone. Disowned and disavowed by one of the most family centered shifter groups in the world. Elephants didn't let elephants go. You were born Herd. You lived Herd. You died Herd. The Herd way was the only way.

Alone.

Free from the responsibility of caring for others. Stop training to be the leader of a Herd. Off the marriage market. Never having to marry some strange bull elephant just to make the Herd happy. Escaping the pressure of becoming the Herd Broodmare.

Freedom.

"Aunt Janet, I'm not saying yes or no, right now. Just let me think about it."

"How long do you need to think?"

Imani scrambled her brains trying to pick a length of time that Aunt Janet would accept. Too long and she would just think Imani was playing and not take her seriously. Too short and the same thing. "Give me until the end of the month."

"End of the month, I'll call back and ask for the last time," Janet said with a finality that would haunt Imani for the rest of her life to come.

"Aunt Janet."

"Yes, Imani?" her aunt said reluctantly.

"Please don't tell my mother."

"I wouldn't dare tell anyone. It won't be me. I don't want to be blamed for your going AWOL from Herd duties and Herd life. It is a reflection on me that you, *you* will be the one to break their hearts. I'll leave that to you to announce it to the Herd." Janet disconnected the phone call without a goodbye.

Imani wished for a moment that she was in Atlanta, at her grandparents' house so that she could be on her grandmother's heavy house phone with its long curly cord. The heavy weight of the receiver would give her so much satisfaction as she slammed the receiver into its cradle. Right now, she only had her smartphone which with her elephant strength if she mashed the screen too hard in her anger, she would obliterate the glass.

Chapter Four

Alpha Meeting

Marshall, Texas is a small town with delusions of being a large city. Imani had searched for any of the home decor stores she was accustomed toto and none of them were in Marshall. She drove to Longview, a larger city thirty minutes to the west of Marshall. She would have to plan a much longer trip to Dallas a couple of hours away to visit the national chain stores, but she would hold that off until she settled into a new apartment.

Her shopping took roughly two hours. She debated over her choice of rug, but finally just followed the advice of Aunt Jasmine even though everything in her wanted to ignore her aunt's advice. The rich ruby red rug would complement more with her light pine and blond wood furniture, but the bronze rug was subtler with an intricate pattern and was more her style. On top of all that, the damn thing was on sale. She was sure her aunt failed to mention that tidbit on purpose knowing Imani had her grandfather's penchant for pinching a penny until Abe Lincoln cried out in alarm.

As she hopped back into her car, she pulled out her large to-do list. Without even realizing it, she had written the name of Coach Harrison's Alpha onto her list. She checked her watch, then her GPS and decided to crash the werewolf chapter meeting. After her last phone call, she could do with some sparring. She hoped the Alpha of the Marshall Werewolf pack liked a good fight. She was ready to shed her human skin and brawl.

Thirty minutes and she was back on the outskirts of Marshall.

One wrong turn later, she pulled up to a large custom-built log mansion. Imani's eyes popped at the seven-story log cabin composed of sixteen-inch-thick logs with a full wraparound porch, four car garages, and a towering river stone fireplace. The house dwarfed her Herd's Atlanta McMansion as she turned her head to see that the house sprawled outward with two separate L wings jutting off the back side.

"Apparently, wolves do it big in Texas."

She headed up the stairs to the front door. Before she could raise her hand to knock, the door opened slowly. Her new nemesis, Coach Harrison stood there with an older woman who he resembled especially around the mouth and jaw line.

"I'm Ada Harrison," Ada declared, reaching a small dark brown hand out to Imani. "My son told me what happened today. I would like to extend apologies on behalf of the entire Harrison family for his behavior. He didn't know who you were."

Imani could hear the rest of the unspoken sentence, 'he didn't know who your family was...'

Deflated, she knew there would be no sparring with this polite lady present. Her aura was virtually pulsing with emotion, embarrassment and regret foremost among them. Imani shook Ada's hand. "Nice to meet you, Ms. Ada. I'm sorry it had to be under these circumstances."

Ada smiled showing deep dimples. "Come in, I'm glad to meet you. Have you had dinner?"

Imani's stomach chose that moment to let out an elephant sized growl that could have been heard without the benefit of shifter hearing. Imani could smell half a dozen food scents in the air and they all smelled tantalizing.

Ada smiled, but didn't comment. "Come along, I'll make you a plate. You can eat and then meet the Alphas." Ada led the way to a commercial sized kitchen fully stocked with high end commercial appliances like the Vulcan double ovens that she recognized from seeing the exact same model in her aunt's bakery. The eat-in kitchen had a full set of luxury furniture including a twelve-person farmhouse table complete with padded benches and damask covered chairs. A hutch laden with china sat behind the table and dominated one entire wall. There was even a small seating area with a concrete coffee table and leather recliners.

"Alphas?" Imani questioned.

"Yes, you chose a good night to come. It is the quarterly Alpha Council meeting tonight. Most of the Alphas in this area are here tonight."

After the Great Shifter War ended, Alphas of all shifter species were mandated to meet quarterly in local Councils by local area, yearly by the state, every two years by region and twice a decade nationwide. Every twenty-five years, there was to be a global Alpha convention, but Imani was very young during the last one and preparations for the next one in four years were underway. These meetings were designed to ease tensions between local shifter groups, air any grievances, and foster a spirit of cooperation. Any shifter was free to attend the Alpha Council meetings locally and state, but most didn't bother. They were often like a local city council meeting, attendance was sparse until something controversial came up then they were packed to the rafters and contentious displays of political naivety and emotional appeals.

Imani had been to the large National Alpha convention only twice. She had acted as a body woman following her grandmother Seraphine and her mother Josephine around carrying their bags, taking notes, collecting all the business cards that the thousands of Alphas in attendance thrust upon them. The national Alpha conference was more of a networking event than the legislative session it was intended during the treaty process to be. As part of her Alpha training she had attended dozens of local and state meetings.

At the six-eyed gas range, Ada began taking the lids off pots and pans and making Imani a plate. The plate she used was a fourteen-inch oval, more of a platter than an actual plate. That didn't stop Ada from filling every inch of space. While she continued to load the plate full of deliciousness, Coach Harrison indicated with a flat hand that she should take a seat at the granite island. He held the barstool out for her. He walked to a mahogany sideboard coming back with a bamboo placemat, a silver charger, a dark blue cloth napkin and full set of silverware like a Downton Abbey footman. He placed everything quickly in front of her before leaving and coming back with a water glass filled with ice, and a thin slice of lemon floating on top. "Would you like wine or..." he whispered.

"Don't be afraid to speak now, Temple," Ada reprimanded. "You didn't have any trouble speaking earlier, did ya?" She turned from the range and seared him with a short look that raised the hairs on Imani's arm. Ms. Ada was a full blown and powerful Alpha werewolf. She hid it well under her Laura Ashley style flower printed dress, full body apron and sensible shoes, but that woman's powers packed enough punch to make the elephant perk up from her slumber. Imani had heard that werewolves often had more than one person capable of being an Alpha but hadn't believed the rumors. The urban legend was true. She needed to call her grandfather to tell him. He would not believe it.

The thought of multiple Alphas in a Herd set Imani's mind to blazing. There had never been more than one Alpha per generation. One woman to lead that whole generation and prepare for the next generation. What next male War Elephants and male elephant Alphas? Inside, Imani could feel her 'phant scoffing herself to tears laughing.

"No, ma'am," he replied to his mother looking as sheepish as an adult man could get. He turned back to Imani and in a stronger voice said, "There is coffee, sweet tea, or lemonade. There's also a full bar if you would prefer something stronger, Coach Wilson."

"Is it possible to get two shots of bourbon mixed with lemonade?"

"Sure, I'll make it myself." He smiled, looking devilishly handsome, and left.

Imani wished she had met the friendly, smiling Temple first.

With a wicked gleam in her eye, Ada delivered Imani's platter. Overflowing with two large pieces of smothered chicken with light brown gravy oozing down the sides and two large, two-inch thick bone in smothered pork chops with a different mushroom gravy covering the tops of both, fat quarter-sized red beans ascending up a mound of fluffy white rice, a bushel of crispy fried cabbage, glistening honey glazed carrots, a mountain of fresh peas, huge wedges of baked macaroni and cheese with bits of bacon and broccoli baked inside, and two grenade-sized golden brown yeast rolls and two fist sized hunks of cornbread — one plain, one with red and green specks.

"Wow!" Imani grabbed her fork and dug in. She ate methodically and quickly, concentrating only on her food and satiating her hunger. Only when the platter held bones and little two pieces of elbow macaroni that Imani couldn't force herself to eat, did she sit back. She grabbed her napkin, gently wiping her mouth and fingers.

She leaned back in the chair, noticing for the first time that she had crept forward hovering over the platter. Even the most even-tempered shifter sometimes exhibited animal behavior around food. Crowding the plate and ignoring everything around them happened too often for it to even become an issue in Shifter society where manners and civility were stressed first and foremost. Remembering her manners, Imani thanked Ada for the amazing feast.

"Seconds?" Ada asked happily. She seemed to beam brighter under Imani's praise for the food. "I made enough to feed a dozen Alphas and only nine showed up."

"God no." Imani reached for her water glass and drained it. "I'm so full you might have to roll me out. Wait, did you say you cooked all of this?" She waved her hand at the empty platter. She picked up the lemonade and bourbon and sipped slowly. It went down smoothly, the sweet lemonade hiding the burn of the mellow bourbon.

"Yes, I'm the chef for the whole lodge," she said as she finished scooping, from the smell of it, freshly ground coffee into an industrial-sized coffee machine.

"This is a lodge? I thought this was someone's home."

Ada chortled as she reached across the island to grab Imani's plate and rinsed it off before placing it in the dishwasher alongside nine others. "The lodge is one of our biggest pack-owned businesses. It was built by our werewolf pack. We hold events here, but we also rent it out to other shifters for meetings and events. This weekend we are hosting a bear wedding for three hundred."

"Wow, three hundred bears! You aren't cooking for all those bears alone, are you?" Imani asked, thinking she may need to volunteer to come help chop veggies to pay for her gourmet soul food meal. Chopping vegetables and kneading bread being the extent of her culinary skills. She had learned during her childhood spent following her aunt around the bakery that those in the kitchen got to eat whatever wasn't going on a plate or in a bag. If Ada cooked like this all the time, Imani needed to find a way to live in this kitchen.

"Heavens no, I have a regular staff of five people and a dozen more temporaries that I can bring in to assist me. If nothing else, I've got seven sons who will pitch in." She began loading a rolling cart with several cakes, pies and brownies, and Imani's eyes got wider. Even though her hopes for kitchen invites were completely dashed. "There is a staff of forty who work here both full and part time. Besides the meetings and events, we offer fishing and hunting tours, and one of my nieces leads a photo safari out on the lakes and marshes for bird watchers and nature photographers. We couldn't run the place without everyone in the Pack chipping in."

Ada finished loading the desserts and gestured to Imani. "Follow me, I'll bring you to meet the other Alphas and you can have dessert with them."

Imani stood, dusted herself off. Suddenly very glad she had changed out of her track suit that she wore to work earlier. She always had the worst timing when it came to her wardrobe. Often finding herself chronically underdressed or overdressed when meeting important Alphas and clans. Her polo shirt, skirt and flats would have to suffice.

Imani hurried to follow the petite chef down several hallways filled with artisan-crafted furniture and crowded with artwork from paintings to sculptures, each with discreet price tags next to them. Imani's mind flitted to the two artisans in her Herd and wondered how much they would benefit from having a permanent gallery like a hotel or bed and breakfast to display their artwork. Something she should talk over with her mother and Aunt Janet, then she remembered Janet's call earlier asking if she was a Rogue.

If she went rogue, then she wouldn't have a say in the next business the Herd invested in. She wouldn't have a say in anything

Herd. Could she go the rest of her life alone? No family. No cousins. No Aunts. No grandparents. No Mom. Her heart started beating triple time.

Ada stopped before a set of ornately carved double doors and knocked gently. Imani pulled up short moments before bumping into Ada. So, lost in her thoughts, she had lost track of where they were heading or even why she was going there. It took her a few seconds to snap back to reality.

"Smells like dessert has arrived," a deep male voice said, "Ada, get in here girl. I was starting to feel peevish. You know I need to eat every two hours."

Ada opened both doors with a flourish and rolled the cart into the room. A young werewolf who looked just like Ada Harrison, detached himself from the wall and began assisting Ada in delivering the dessert cart around.

"Alphas, I would like to present Imani Wilson, daughter of Josephine and granddaughter of Seraphine," Ada said in a feminine boom that would have made majordomos across the world proud.

Ada stepped to the side so that Imani could walk through the open doors. Imani stood in front a semi-circle table surrounded by Alpha shifters. Some of the shifters were in their prime early forties to mid-sixties. Others were younger, early thirties, and a couple like the grey-haired lady were well past their prime in their seventies and eighties.

"To what do we owe the pleasure of having the granddaughter of the Great Seraphine attend our humble local Alpha Council?"

Imani inhaled deeply. The room was bursting with the scents of fur, hide, feathers, scales, something wet and something metallic that she couldn't quite place. Imani beamed. This was the shifter diversity that she had been searching for this morning in the Wiley College dining hall. After living her whole life in Atlanta surrounded by shifters of every variety from small to large, Imani had feared being stuck in a small town with only elephants and wolves.

"I have recently taken a position in the area and wanted to introduce myself to you all. I also have a personal matter with the

Alpha of the werewolves that I need to address as well."

"How is Sera?" the matriarch inquired. Only true-blue friends who knew her grandmother intimately dared to shorten her name. The rest of the world only called her Seraphine. She was like Cher or Oprah that way.

Imani could feel power radiate off her in ripples. It was just like being in the room with her grandmother. Too much power couldn't be contained in their human or animal form. Many, but not all, Alpha's powers continued to grow the older they became until they were unable to keep the power under wraps. Imani dreaded the day her own powers expanded. She was already more powerful than all her aunts and her mother and very close to the level of her grandmother's considerable powers. Her grandmother had stopped working hard to keep from sucking people into the gravitational pull of her Alpha powers. She just trampled her way through life and local shifters just learned to get out of her way.

"She is well. She has recently retired." Which Imani had realized with the help her friends, Davida and Lillian, was the reason her mother and aunts were trying to marry her off and have her start popping calves out as fast as she could.

"Please send her my regards."

"Yes, ma'am. May I have your information to pass on?"

"Of course."

Imani had wanted the lady's cell phone information, but the Alpha was old school and Imani felt the fission of power come for her. She locked her knees expecting the power to hit her like a freight train. Then she would end up prostrate on the floor like Coach Harrison had this morning. Which would be karmic justice if nothing else. Instead it curled around her like a comfy sweater with a warm breeze.

"Greetings from Louise Levanger," it whispered. That tendril of power also had Ms. Louise's cell number and other information in it.

Imani was impressed, tucking away the tendril until later when she could pass the information to her grandmother. She was going home later to practice adding her contact information into her powers. When you pack as much Alpha power as an elder anyway to use it up was welcomed.

"Now that you have met Louise, I'm Dexter Waycross, Alpha of the Werewolves." Dexter was a lean man with terra cotta coloring, skinny pencil sized dreadlocks to his shoulders and a predatory grin flashing white teeth a quarter inch gap between his two front teeth. He looked like he was wearing two or three layers of clothing and still could hoola-hoop a Cheerio. She would have to ask Henrietta or someone later about Dexter's strange orange coloring.

He gestured to his left and went down the table. "This is Destiny Flores, she is Alpha of the Javelina."

Imani made a mental note to go home and look up what a javelina was in the Encyclopedia of Shifters that the Grand Council of Shifters put out every decade.

"Pleasure to meet you, Ms. Flores."

She was a Chicano woman with long, dark hair in a fat braid that fell over her shoulder and disappeared beneath the table. Her dark eyes flashed in her J-Lo shaped face. "Destiny is fine."

Dexter continued, "This is Henrietta Marvin, she is the..."

"Dexter, Imani and I have met previously," Henrietta interrupted. She smiled gently at Imani. "How are you feeling?"

"Much better, thanks to your delicious baked goods."

Dexter's head swiveled between the two werelephants waiting for a chance to finish the introductions.

Henrietta smiled, but said nothing further.

"Next to Henrietta is..."

"Professor Junaid," Imani finished for Dexter.

"Dexter, Imani and I had the pleasure of meeting this morning at Wiley."

Something about the way Ansel said her name stirred a reaction in Imani down to her core. She breathed slowly not wanting her reaction to him to be obvious. All the small hairs on her body stood at attention. Maybe, Davida was right again. She should have some fun with Ansel. Just being the object of his piercing stare got her all verklempt.

Dexter continued with the introductions, but the name of the other four Alphas went in one ear and out the other. All she could think about was Ansel saying her name and the promise of pleasure in his voice.

Her mind flashed with images of Ansel's large hands rubbing her thighs while they kissed. His large body lifting her lightly off the ground to sit on a kitchen counter while they kissed long and deep. Her legs wrapped around his waist as they struggle to take each other's clothes off while still trying to keep their lips locked. That was a scene from a movie that she always wanted a boyfriend to reenact.

Chapter Five

You're The Next Contestant on The….

"**A**ntsy, you're' the Alpha of the largest group of shifters in the world. It is imperative that you allow the security guards to do their jobs and keep you safe. You can't just take off and be alone..."

Ansel rubbed his hand over the length of his face and head as he listened to his mother drone on about his security. He had heard this exact same line of conversation from her only a few dozen hundred thousand times since was ten. Twenty-five years of "Must be safe. Must not risk himself. Must be protected." was wearing him down. His mother still treated him like he wasn't a fully-fledged and blooded Alpha, completely capable of fighting his own battles against any enemy.

His mother, Kathleen, continued her lecture, but not in the same vein that he was accustomed to.

"Furthermore, the end of your Claiming Time is quickly approaching. Too quickly and you have waited way too long." She paused her flow of words, and Ansel's trouble antennae went up. If she wasn't his mother, he would have used his Alpha voice to command her confession.

"What have you done, Mother?" He was resigned enough at this point to just follow through with it. Whatever it was couldn't be that bad.

"Six months ago, I sent out fifty nomination requests to the upper reaches of shifter society. I asked they submit names of eligible ladies to meet you," his mother said quietly.

Simultaneously, all the blood drained from his head while his blood pressure spiked. "You did WHAT? Mother, I'm not a rare handbag that you can sell discreetly to a certain class of people!"

"Your Betas, Cheryl, and I went through the nominations carefully and selected the crème de la crème."

"You involved my Betas." Ansel's voice crackled. Static electricity building around him. He felt the impundulu's anger spike alongside his own. Not only had his mother interfered in his search for a mate, but she involved his people. The people he commanded, who looked to him to lead. She had diminished his authority in the eyes of his people.

Even worse, they had all kept secrets from him letting him walk into this trap of his mother's with no warning. Even his twin sister, Cheryl had said nothing to him. They two of them were going to have a long talk. He guessed Cheryl went along because she was even more afraid for his safety than their mother, but a hint that they were trying to matchmake would have gone a long way.

"I've set up seven dates for you in the next week. I chartered a private plane to bring them to Marshall. I worked with Ada Harrison to rent the top floor of the lodge for them to stay for a week while you meet with them. There will be a few group dates — a fishing excursion, a photo safari in the 'wilds' of East Texas, a trip to the rodeo, and a reading by that author you love with the wild hair. Then each lady and you will have a private meal every night of the week," his mother said in a rush as if hoping to get it all out before Ansel could object.

"Mother! Are you putting cameras in too and filming for your own version of The Bachelor: Shifter Edition?" Ansel sighed in exasperation. He put the phone on speaker and laid his head down on the cool surface of his kitchen peninsula, letting the coolness of the granite seep into the side of his heated face. He really wanted to hang up the phone or throw it across the room.

He could do neither; his mother was right. He needed a mate now. No N, more like he needed her two years ago when his own inborn magic had started to wane signaling the beginning of his claiming time.

A vision of Imani almost running away from him that first morning in line for coffee sprang to mind. He felt his animal shift from anger to sexual frustration and deep resignation at thoughts of Imani. The animal whimpered with pain that she didn't seem as interested in them as they were in her. Their first two interactions so far had proved deflating. Imani would see him, he would get just a moment to glimpse her heart-shaped face and those electric amber eyes, then all he would get would be the back of her as she smoothly navigated away from him. The back of her was just as gorgeous as the front with her long shapely legs and wide hips. He could easily be hypnotized just watching her fierce sashay away from him, her hips swinging side to side.

He had spent the next week haunting the coffee kiosk every morning, so he could buy her that muffin and coffee. Eventually, he discovered through Keisha, the barista that Imani was busy early morning mornings training the soccer team. Several times in the last week, he had thought of storming the gym or soccer field. Imani and her elephant clearly weren't their mate, or she wouldn't leave the room as if she was on fire and all the water was outside. She left within minutes of them being around each other. That hadn't stopped her from invading his thoughts these last couple of weeks and taking up permanent residence in his dreams. Imani was the star of the wettest, hottest most erotic dreams he'd ever had. He reached down to adjust himself. Thoughts of Imani bringing an immediate erection.

"No. However, that is a very good idea," Kathleen continued slower this time as if she sensed his defeat through the phone. "The ladies will arrive on Friday night from..." she paused. He could picture her running her dark index finger down a set of papers on a clipboard, consulting her itinerary. His mother was a list maker. She had lists of her lists. "Shreveport airport. Your fishing excursion will be at six a.m. Saturday morning with Bull Harrison. Ada will serve a light breakfast before and a full breakfast after. Your sister is going to arrive with the ladies and run logistics for me. Unfortunately, due to some other work obligations; I won't arrive until Monday afternoon."

Thank heavens for small miracles, Ansel thought. He couldn't imagine meeting seven potential mates with both his mother and sister and a crowd of local shifters and whoever else was at the Lodge for the weekend watching.

"I love you, Antsy."

"I love you too, Mom," he replied automatically.

"This is for the best. We have to get you settled. I've taken care of everything else. All you need to do is pick the best lady of the bunch. Good night."

"Goodnight, Mom. Thanks for all your hard work." Ansel said the words, but the last thing he felt was grateful; he felt more like he was in a coffin and the lid was closing.

His mother hurried off the phone smoothly avoiding his losing his temper all over her like a spilled glass of milk. Somehow his mother had gotten her way, Ansel was going to pick a wife. A wife his mother and Betas had chosen, not the mate of his dreams.

His smartphone blinked a new message icon just as his mother disconnected. He thumbed the screen to read, "I'm coming. Your soul will be mine."

He did drop the phone then, the screen shattering against the sharp edge of the kitchen granite counter.

Chapter Six
Hacker

She laughed. The sound was creaky, and rust covered. She paused, she wasn't sure the last time she was this amused, but watching the Alpha drop his phone in panic at her text was the funniest thing she had witnessed in some decades. She should have been born a shifter, a cat, a really large cat with claws, a lion or tiger. She always like to play with her food before she devoured it.

Turning from the computer screen. "Everything is coming along…" she pronounced. She patted the shoulder of the young hacker. The spell she prepared earlier transferring from her hand to him. Wiping his memory of hacking the Impundulu and his family's phones and computers just like he had wiped his computer monitor off with a rag.

His last week would be blank. No witch or wizard alive could return these memories.

Chapter Seven
Time is Of The Essence

Ansel awoke to the sound of discreet knocking on his bedroom door. Groaning, he sat up throwing the covers off and stood heading for the door. He yanked the door open to find his best friend and head of his security team, Stanley Washington with his fist upraised for another round of knocking.

"Sorry to wake you, but we can't find anything on the phone."

Before Ansel could ask, Stanley continued, "Our techs tried to trace the SMS message, but need more time."

Ansel sighed. He refrained from yelling at Stan with the hardest grip on his temper. None of this was his fault "Then why did you wake me up?"

Stan finally explained, "I woke you because your mother and sister received messages taunting them about 'how you would no longer be a member of the family' and that they needed to say their goodbyes."

"Who the hell *is* this? How do they have not only my number, but all my family's numbers?"

"We don't know, but I'm going to find out. I guarantee," Stan said with a feral gleam in his yellow eyes. Stanley stood five feet eleven inches and carried muscles over his wiry frame like a welter weight boxer with heavy shoulder muscles and thick cut abdominals that you could bounce bricks off. He had all of the conviction a panther shifter could muster. Stanley liked nothing better than to have something to hunt and pounce on with fists or paws. If left to his own devices, Stanley would spend more time in the jungle covered in his fur than in his human skin.

"I'm canceling this whole group date, instant mate shenanigans."

"Ansel, your mother and I both advises against it. These messages prove more than ever you need a mate now. We can't lose you."

Chapter Eight
Four Score and A Boar

"Hello?" Imani answered groggily, pulling her cell off the charger. She sat up in bed tossing the heavy crimson duvet off before the warmth of the bed dragged her back to dreamland.

"Good morning, Imani! It's Henrietta. Sorry for calling unannounced and so early. but it just occurred to me. I was wondering if you would like to come out with our Herd this morning for a Walk? We normally assemble before dawn, Commune, then go out to breakfast."

Imani stifled a yawn. "That sounds lovely." The elephant loved nothing more than a good Walk.

"Great! I'll have one of my nieces' text you the directions. See you in a bit." The call ended.

Henrietta was way too perky for — Imani turned her head toward the digital clock on her bedside table and rolled her amber eyes — four seventeen a.m. on a Saturday morning. Imani yawned again, a jaw cracking, mouth wide open head thrown all the way back yawn. She had slept pretty well, but she hadn't planned on getting only four hours and seventeen minutes of sleep when she tucked herself into bed at midnight. Reluctantly stopping her Netflix only when she finished the last season of a detective series and couldn't decide on what to begin bingeing next.

She felt the warmth of the covers disappearing around her. There was just enough residual heat left in the sheets to lull her back to a deep sleep, but her elephant's excitement was too high about shifting and communing with other elephants. She wouldn't even allow her to think about crawling back under the covers.

She was up, moving about and dressed in a faded Clark Atlantic tank top, old loose-fitting gray sweats that needed to be headed to the closet in the sky instead of outside to be seen, and her flip flops before she even realized it. When the bell tolling her text notification came through, she was standing at her front door with keys in hand, purse on her shoulder and butterflies in her stomach.

Navigating the outside staircase and hoping not to trip and fall with her still sleeping brain; she made her way to her car. The drive to where the Marshall Herd communed was fifteen minutes away according to GPS. She debated hitting a drive through for coffee and a sausage biscuit.

It took Imani thirty minutes to find the driveway entrance for the private land where the Marshall Herd communed. She had passed the unmarked driveway twice in the darkness before finally the 'phant got frustrated with Imani's inability to spot it and turned in. There were over two dozen cars assembled in a semicircular, white gravel lot. Just as Imani turned the engine off, another car's headlights flickered across her rearview mirror.

At least I'm not the last one to get here and won't have to use my church finger as I sneak in the back. Imani chuckled to herself.

She got out of her car and followed the path through the trees toward the sounds of murmuring voices. As she approached a larger, grassy clearing, she looked around for Henrietta, Coach Henry or even the real estate agent niece, Veronica who had texted her.

Before she could approach the center of the Herd, a young slender bull turned to her menacingly. He was her age. Late twenties, mahogany skin, huge dimple on the left side of his face. He was shirtless and carried no discernable fat anywhere her eyes could see because his low-slung grey sweatpants hid nothing. Davida would label him on her scale of hawtness "smoking hawt." The only thing above smoking was volcanic. Imani had personally given that volcanic label to one political science professor although she would never tell Davida.

"This is private land. Visitors aren't welcome." He continued stalking toward her until he was directly in her face. Their noses inches from touching.

What is it about these male Texas shifters that kept them running up on her and challenging her? she thought to herself.

"Well then lucky for me I. Was. Invited," she said the last three words through clenched teeth, unfurling her full Alpha power like a raging tsunami in his direction. Her elephant was so close to the skin, one wayward breeze would cause her to shift and gore whatever or whoever was in her path.

The small bull stepped back twice as the immensity of her powers hit him full force. He didn't bow as he ought, but Imani looked forward to making him submit to her fully another time.

Henrietta forced her way through, appearing from out of the crowd. Henrietta's powers fully extended also, but her powers paled in comparison to the sheer immensity of Imani's. Her powers were a trickle of a stream compared to the ocean of Imani. Undeterred, Henrietta kept radiating peaceful tones toward both Imani and the bull. "Victor, how dare you insult our guest this way!" Her tone even though peaceful, promised retribution later for Victor.

"Everyone, this is Imani, daughter of Josephine, granddaughter of the Great Seraphine, The War Elephant, The Matriarch Loxodonta Africana Homosapien. She recently moved here to Marshall. Imani also works with our Henry at Wiley. I invited her to Commune with us this morning."

All eyes snapped back to Imani. There was a murmur that passed over the Marshall Herd. Everyone gathered in the field inclined their head toward her. Some she could feel the respect radiating from them, but from the others pure terror. Other's stares were just as judgmental as she was used to from shifters of all shapes and sizes. Her grandmother's role in the Great War was controversial and was still disputed publicly in the halls of government and privately around kitchen tables thirty years later. The Matriarch War Elephant had both loyal advocates and fierce opponents.

Inwardly, Imani cringed. She had felt a lifetime of judgmental stares start as soon as her grandmother's name was brought up in conversation. It couldn't be helped that her grandmother was the most famous elephant shifter in several generations. No, she was the most famous shifter ever. She stopped a world war thrusting the entire shifter and magical community out of the dark and hidden places into the world's society.

However, Grand had told her long ago as a child, she never had to worry about fulfilling some legacy only about finding her own happiness, but that didn't stop others from expecting more from her or judging her before she even opened her mouth.

Imani's elephant was fighting to get out. Her 'phant loathed being stared at by anyone. A whole Herd looking at her was just asking for trouble. She could feel her thick elephant hide pressed tightly against her skin pushing its way out. Her feet, hands and everything else was slowly swelling. Her human body was fighting a losing battle trying to contain the elephant's soul and fury.

"Harriet, why don't you begin the ceremony?"

A pear-shaped woman with skin the color of butter pecan ice cream sang the opening refrain of the Communal Song. It was a call and response song very similar to something heard in a Baptist church, but it carried the sounds of the Savanna and longing and heartache calling to the inner Loxodonta Africana inside all of them. The nearly forty shifters raised their voices echoing the longing for the scorching hot sun, the whisper of tall grasses, the bird song and so much more.

As the song climaxed and died, everyone begins to wordlessly undress and shift. As the Herd's Alpha, it was Henrietta's job to lead the Herd on its communal walk. Imani shifted allowing her animal out finally. As her four feet touched the short dewy grass of the land, Imani dragged her toes into the land, dirtying her toenails. She shook her head, flapping her ears. She breathed deep of the pre-dawn air expelling it through her trunk and mouth. Hoping to get her elephant adjusted to its new home quicker.

She could feel some of the anxiety slough off her back and sides. Nothing soothed her like being on four feet.

The Atlanta Herd's Communal walk was normally between a seven to ten mile amble through the woods to a large creek. At the creek, the little calves would frolic in and around the water and the mothers and fathers would lounge on the bank. After a few hours they would walk back to their starting point. Following that second amble, they would shift back to human. Then collectively go to one of the Herd owned restaurants normally a buffet and eat until they were all stuffed like they partook in the best Thanksgiving meal.

Commune Day was a day for lounging and eating and more lounging. At home, sometimes they would all go to one of the aunts' house and sleep for several hours in one big pile. Then they would wake up, order several dozen pizzas and watch movies still entangled together.

Henrietta didn't mention the length of the walk or whether she was available. If Imani's brain hadn't been pre-coffee she might have remembered to ask. As it was, she was just honored and thrilled to be invited. Just like her Herd she assumed that most of these 'phants were related either by blood or marriage. It wasn't very often that her own Herd would invite an outsider to join for Commune Day. Thinking back, she could only remember twice that her Herd had hosted visitors.

She would have to apologize later to Henrietta when they found themselves alone for bringing unneeded drama and unwanted strife to her Herd gathering. Henrietta led the elephants walking in mainly a straight, single file line. Following Henrietta were the oldest females, then younger females with calves, female cows with no calves, then married bulls with single bulls bringing up the rear. Imani took her place as the first of the female cows with no calves. The calves were always in the center of the Herd for protection. The littles holding onto their mother's tails with their trunks. In the wild, bull males often left or were pushed out of the Herd. Among shifters, unmarried bull shifters stayed with their maternal Herd until they married and went to their wife's Herd.

Her own trunk had the mind of a toddler calf this morning. It touched the bark of every tree and each stone or rock in reach. Learning the scents, texture and shape of everything it touched. Somewhere near mile six, her 'phant scented water. It was still a couple of miles away and moving at a pretty fast clip, but Imani breathed another sigh of relief.

Three miles later, the Herd ambled up to a pristine sandy beach on a clear lake surrounded by more of the dense forest of ash, oak, pine and elm. Most of the littles went straight for the bright blue water. Some of the older calves went for giant tractor tire swings that had been mounted on concrete pillars. Even more 'phants went toward what looked like a football field sized mud pit. The older women and men picked out spots stretching out across the sand like pearls on a giant, gray necklace. Imani went alone further down the sandy stretch of beach looking for a place large enough for her 'phant to stretch all the way out so she could roll in the sand easing what felt like hundreds of itchy places on her hide with the coarse sand before she too went into the water. Just like in her human size, Imani's 'phant was bigger than almost everyone in attendance.

As she stretched out, she missed the playful way someone would blow sand over her. Being out here under the clear Texas sky and bright early morning sun, Imani was hit with the biggest bout of homesickness she'd experienced in the last three weeks. She realized how much she missed her mother, grandmother and grandfather and her aunts. Before they could be stopped, tears streamed out of her eyes and down her trunk. Crying soundlessly, she rolled over in the sandy bank twice completely covering her hide in the white sand of the lake's beach.

Slowly she lumbered her bulk up out of the depression in the sand she had carved out with her 'phant's bulk. Just as she was heading to the cool water of the lake, she felt pelted with sand. A trumpet of elephant calls sounded as she shook her head and chuffed at most of the littles and Henrietta and Henry and several other adults who had blown sand all over her. She trumpeted back her laughter, sucked sand up her trunk and blew it all at the cutest little one, a girl calf who had run closest to her. All the littles scattered back to playing while the other adults moved on and Henrietta soothed her trunk over the clefts of Imani's head.

After Henrietta spent a few moments comforting her, they both headed into the chilly water. The cute little calf she had blown sand at came swimming right to her. She pointed to the other side of the lake with her trunk to a rock that jutted over the lake. She mimed a few movements with her trunk. It took Imani a couple of moments, but she finally got it.

That large rock was like a diving board. The little one ran off and Imani gave chase around the sharp bend in the lake. If the little one was in human form, she would be giggling her little head off the whole way there. They reached the incline at the same time. The little girl calf found a set of smaller boulders that looked like they had been levered into place for this purpose. The calf climbed onto Imani's broad back. After she settled, she gave a little beep of sound that sounded like a ready to Imani.

Imani backed up twenty paces then as fast as she could, charged up the incline and across the large rock. She didn't slow for one second. At the end, she spread her feet out and soared for a few blissful seconds that felt like forever. She hung airborne before she belly-flopped into the lake thirty feet below. The splash the two of them created was still rising into the cloudless sky when Imani's head and trunk surfaced.

The little calf had soared further out than Imani. She must have used her back as a springboard to leap even further than Imani's charge had taken them. The fearless little calf swam past Imani right for the shore at a pretty fast speed. As her feet touched the shore, something dark and bullet shaped came hurtling out of the dense woods right toward them. Imani dove onto the shore, her trunk shoving the little calf back toward the lake.

Instinct took over, she lowered her head. Her body responded to the danger automatically, her fourth and most deadly shape emerged. Her second and third set of tusks emerged. Then all three sets elongated curving upwards to deadly points like a scimitar sword. Her already thick hide grew denser covering her whole body with scales that looked like impenetrable plate armor.

As the shape came hurtling closer, it revealed itself to be a feral, massively overgrown razorback. It stood five and a half feet tall at the shoulder with huge two-foot-long curved tusks. It didn't appear to slow down at all even with the larger threat of Imani in its way. It headed directly at where the little calf had been before Imani's trunk had twisted out and shoved her safely behind her. Without pausing, Imani charged the razorback putting herself between it and the calf who was still trying to peek around her legs.

She judged the speed it was traveling, lowered her head and scored both lower sets of her tusks down its right flank. Scoring deep twin grooves into its hairy black hide. The razorback bled freely staining the sand of the lake a dark crimson. She wheeled back around in a tight turn, well as tight a turn as a charging twenty-ton war-elephant could make. The creature was just barely standing, listing to its injured side, but it was still enraged and pumped up with the thrill of hunting. The elephant could hear its heart beating erratically as it tried to compensate for the blood lost. It didn't know it was dead, even still standing on its feet. For safe measure, Imani scored her lower tusks down its uninjured left side.

Imani slowed her charge. She checked where the little calf was standing. Thankfully she was still by the water line. Scanning the rest of the line of trees with her eyes, Imani's expanded senses looking for other razorbacks and other threats.

Her heart was going a thousand miles an hour. She could feel her heartbeat from the tip of her trunk to the end of her now spiked tail. She shifted back to human. Electric sparks were dancing in front of her eyes. Her breathing was ragged like she ran all the way home to Georgia and back.

She tried walking in circles to calm herself down, but she would need to walk to the moon and back to work off the adrenaline coursing through her veins. She stalked over to the razorback guarding her kill from harming anyone else or from anyone else taking it. She walked circles around it as it shuddered its last few breathes. Both her and the razorback's sides were heaving and their heads twitching. She stared at its eyes from every angle as she paced faster and faster. Her senses were so charged, she felt like she could see its last breath as a puff on the wind. Imani even watched until its eyes turned glassy as she stared.

The little calf came trotting up finally. She still had no fear in her eyes as if she wasn't in any danger and hadn't ever been in any danger. Or maybe she just expected Imani to protect her while in her human form too. The rest of the Herd arrived while she was trying to keep the curious calf back from the sharp tusks.

The calf's mother put her trunk on the back of her neck and pushed down gently. Forcing her to submit and shift back.

All the Marshall Herd shifted back to human around them.

Coach Henry came jogging up. He looked at the corpse of the razorback with its deep twin gouges down the side. Then he looked to Imani, then back at the corpse. Finally, he shook his graying head. "Well, I'll be damned." Speechless, he stood watching the razorback.

Imani continued to pace, trying to work off the adrenaline coursing through her veins like she shot herself up with three gallons of Red Bull. She wanted to go run back up that incline and dive off that boulder again and again just to have that weightless sensation of flight.

Henrietta arrived lastly. She shifted. "Young lady, I don't know if I should be angry or relieved."

"I'm grateful!" the calf's mother said. She came up to Henrietta and Imani holding the calf on her hip. "Thank you so much for protecting her! Our Family is in Your Debt," she said in the formal way.

Imani nodded acknowledging. She didn't trust herself to begin speaking as her breathing was still narrowing and broadening. Her heart was like a jackhammer.

"There is no way Vixen would have been able to fight off a fully-grown razorback on her own much less a beast of this size."

Coach Henry asked, "What do you want to do with it?" gesturing to the bristled beast.

"I don't have the slightest idea of what to do. How to clean it. Or cook it. Or anything. I live in apartment. I don't even have freezer space. You can have it!" Imani squeezed out, doing her best Stevie from Malcolm in the Middle impersonation.

"We should cook it today," someone shouted.

"Take it to the processor! Bacon for everyone!" another added.

"How about this? We could take the whole hog over to the Wolf Lodge and get Ada Harrison to roast it in one of their big pits. Since none of us have a pit large enough," Henrietta suggested. "We were headed there afterwards for the breakfast buffet."

"Vernon, go get my truck," Coach Henry called to one of the young bulls. He took off running, morphing from human to elephant as he ran. "Vlad, Vaughn, Vidal, y'all come help lift it so we can rinse some of this blood and sand off."

"You ladies head on back to the driveway. These young bulls and I will meet you at the Lodge." He looked to Henrietta for agreement. At her nod, together, the Marshall Herd and Imani shifted from human to elephant and begin their walk back to the gravel lot.

Chapter Nine
Four Hour Tour

If Ansel could, he would launch himself from the boat right now. He would hide in the clouds or another country until all these ladies, and he used to the term *loosely*, had grown tired and left. He feared no one, but thoughts of his mother's wrath if she found out he had left in the middle of this mating attempt kept him seated, but just barely.

This was a bad idea.

This was a horrible idea.

This was the worst idea his mother had ever had.

He could have told her this was a bad idea before the boat even launched from the dock.

Of course, he could never say that to her. She would never admit it out loud to him, but she had to have known this was going to go badly.

A four-hour long fishing trip in which the only thing he caught was a bad attitude. He hadn't even gotten to cast one line. What was his mother thinking putting such different ladies and types of shifters — a bear, a cheetah, a lion and three birds of prey shifters together in a boat with him?

Shifter women of different species were often catty and competitive when there was nothing to compete for, but with him as the 'prize' for this disaster filled week of dating and mating; these women were in ultimate combat mode.

Already, he had to pull two of the women, Renee and Jessica, away from each other before claws and paws came out as they got into an argument over who was more fertile and willing to give him more cubs or krams. He'd stopped Evelyn, a pouty, potty mouthed bear from feeling up his thigh to his crotch. Pulled multiple fishhooks out of Morgan Murphy McDonald's hand, an injury that he was pretty sure was self-inflicted while she chatted with him about her extensive luxury handbag collection and her luxury cars and her luxury crossbred dog. He'd also been forced to decline two outright offers of marriage, one from Angela who assured him she would earn a seven-figure bonus from her Wall Street banker father and would deem to share parts of the bonus with him. The other one was from Sybil whose offer came with a caveat of open marriage.

All of this before ten a.m. He needed a coffee drip line started, pumping directly in his veins. The cup he half spilled at first breakfast was coming back to haunt him. He was easily three cups of coffee in the morning and two cups in the afternoon type of shifter.

Luckily, the last lady who had been invited didn't show up or it could have been even worse.

He was looking forward to being alone, a stiff drink and food, in that order. He glowered. He could feel their eyes on him as he sat in the back of the boat.

He opened himself up and let his Alpha powers out to keep them away. In his thirty-four years, he only remembered publicly showing his powers and most of those times had been for ceremonial things like being named Alpha Heir, then the later for the actual Alpha naming ceremony when his father was killed. Right now, heh needed the buffer, so he allowed his powers to radiate the frustration he felt. He rarely, no, he never used his powers this way as a shield against the world.

They all sat lined up along the benches like they were outside the principal's office. Defiant not defeated, they would side eye each other. Growls could be heard and felt from of the four-legged type shifters; growls which set all of their nerves on edge.

As the boat pulled alongside the dock, he leaped forward to assist the women getting off the boat.

"I'm sorry, Antsy. This sounded better when Mom came up with the idea," Cheryl said softly as the last of the dates stalked off the boat and down the dock. "You love fishing. Getting them out on the water was supposed to show us their peaceful side. Show them that you aren't a scary Alpha. Give each of you a few moments to talk quietly and get to know one another." Cheryl was on the verge of tears.

"It was a great idea, in theory. However, none of them are the peaceful type," Ansel said laughingly. Grabbing his sister in a rough embrace. "Don't cry, Cantsy. Fate will send me the right mate before my claiming period is up. She'll be beautiful. She'll be strong enough to keep me fighting against the call, but she won't be one of those women."

Bull Harrison leaped on the dock from his thirty-foot boat. He came strolling up with his bandy-legged walk while several young werewolves swarmed the boat lashing her into her place and going aboard to clean and prepare for her next tour.

"Don't think I've ever been out with a group, human, shifter or otherwise and no one came back without a fish," he said without preamble to his long-time fishing buddy, Ansel. "Are you sure you want to be tied to one of those city girls?" Somehow, Bull made city girl sound like both a curse and curse words.

Ansel cracked his first true smile of the morning. "I just told my sister that we have to have faith that Fate is going to send me a mate. Not everyone is as lucky as you and Ada."

Bull smiled at the mention of Ada. "It wasn't always easy. We met at a middle school dance when we were thirteen. One look at her and I knew. My bull knew. When my dad came to pick me up after the dance, he and his bull knew they would have to kill us to keep us apart. Her family and the whole pack got used to the idea after a decade or so. Wolves are a strange lot. After our being together for thirty-seven years now; they are so used to me, they forget I'm not a wolf." He barked a laugh.

Gesturing behind him to the boat as werewolves were following his precise instructions for the care of his watercraft.

Ansel, Cheryl and Bull turned quickly at the sound of running feet on the dock. "Dad, the Elephant Herd just brought in like a thousand-pound razorback they killed. Mom says she needs your help to get the big roasting pit ready." A teenage wolf came running up the gangway.

"Tell her I'm right behind you, Baylor."

Baylor took off, not bothering to even slow down. He ran around the trio heading back the way he had come.

"If you'll excuse me,", Bull started.

"Actually, can we come with you? I've always wanted to see a feral razorback up close." Cheryl asked. "The news always has segments about wild hogs, but I've never seen one."

"Sure," Bull agreed.

"Cheryl, I really just want to eat and go to my room."

"Please, Antsy!" Cheryl begged tugging on his arm and heart strings.

Ansel sighed. He was never able to tell his baby sister no when she called him her pet name and begged.

Before he could even begin to explain how all he craved was privacy; he found himself following Cheryl and Bull Harrison up the dock, across the wide expanse of lawn around the Lodge to an area that looked and smelled like it was more for wolf private parties than for the public guests.

Henry Marvin was backing his custom lifted F-150 up to the loading dock area of the lodge with four young bull elephants riding in the tail area. They all hopped off the back as Henry threw the truck in park. They pushed and shoved to be the one to uncover the razorback for the quickly assembling crowd of wolves and any other curious shifters in the vicinity.

With a rustle, the drop cloth was lifted with little to no fanfare. Everyone gasped at the size of the razorback. He filled the entire bed of Henry's truck side to side and front to back. No wonder the tailgate was down.

Bull Harrison strode straight to the tailgate. He grabbed the wild hog's head lifting it up, judging the weight, before placing it gently back down. "He's a monster! How did you take him down? I thought you elephants didn't hunt…?" Questions bubbled up out of the normally taciturn Bull as he looked in awe at the black furred beast. "Temple, go get the tape. He has to be a record."

A murmur rippled over the crowd as Bull spoke. As the Lodge's Chief Hunter, if Bull was impressed then they all were.

Henry laughed. "We don't have to hunt. Elephants have no natural enemies except dragons. There are barely enough of them to be worth shifting for the fight. We're too large and we travel in herds. Most animals just aren't that foolish." He gestured to the razorback. "This thing came charging out of the forest at our lake. Imani thought he was going for the calf, Vixen. She gored him on one side before the rest of us even sensed the danger. Then she gored him on the other side before any of us got around the lake. He was dead before he hit the ground probably."

"Imani Wilson?" Ansel choked out. His heart jackrabbited at the thought of her in danger and having to defend herself and a baby all alone. "Was she hurt?"

"Nope! She was walking around the kill to make sure it was dead when we got there," one of the young guys said.

"Her elephant is a beast!" another chimed in.

The knot in Ansel's chest loosened at the news that she was unharmed. "Where is she?" he asked Henry.

"Back with the rest of the Herd finishing our Communal. She'll be here later for brunch with everyone," Henry answered nonchalantly.

Ansel started plotting to get Henry to invite him to brunch, Herd or no. Ansel needed to see Imani with his own eyes. It had been ten days since he had laid eyes on her. There was just a glimpse of her jogging around campus through his classroom window. She ran like the wind was chasing her. He had almost stopped his lecture on the dangers of logrolling to chase her.

"Now, Bull, how much are you and Ada going to charge us to roast this bad boy. I know you have to have something large enough to do the job. Cause if you don't, half the Herd wants to take him to the processor and see how much bacon we can get out of him."

Dexter Waycross came striding across the lawn toward the crowd who were crawling around Henry's truck to get a look at the giant razorback.

All the wolves moved six steps back as Dexter approached, the deference due to an Alpha of Dexter's stature. For the millionth time, Ansel wondered why he couldn't sense his powers at all. He never did and never had in the entire time that he'd known the wolf.

Dexter ruled through respect not intimidation. However, the rumor was, in his youth Dexter was such a savage brawler that when he challenged for Alpha six years previously that no one wanted to fight him. Ansel found it hard to believe that in a pack of over two hundred wolves, no one would fight him.

Dexter also had an ace up his sleeve that made him a natural choice for Alpha to his once cash strapped and triple bankrupted werewolf pack. Dexter had just finished an MBA at the University of Texas at Austin. His business savvy had transformed the Marshall Werewolf Pack from a loosely connected family pack of werewolves and their mates to shareholders in a large corporation that was the umbrella group for several businesses with each wolf in the pack steadily building their monetary wealth. In ten years, the Marshall Pack would be the wealthiest werewolves in the nation.

"My, my, my, look what the elephant dragged in," the Alpha wolf said laughingly, as he stepped up on the rear wheel of the truck and looked down into the tailgate at the giant razorback. "When was the last time you had someone clear those woods of yours, Henry? It had to have been a while for this beast to grow so large."

Henry scratched his chin. The scree, scree of his nails across his salt and pepper beard was heard by everyone in the loading area. After a few moments, he shrugged. "I'd have to ask one of my sisters to check the Herd history. It's been at least twenty years maybe longer. You don't think we could have more of them this size in the woods, do you?"

"I should hope not." Dexter paused. A thought occurring to him. "I'd defer to Bull or one of our other seasoned hunter guides to be sure." Gesturing to Bull and a couple of wolves standing near the tailgate. They all nodded together. "If you and Henrietta like, we could offer to lease the land and hunt it for you with our tours. It would triple the amount of hunting grounds we have. I'm sure we could come up with a reasonable split for meat on top of our usage fees we would pay to the Herd and the amount of the yearly lease, of course." Dexter grinned wolfishly. "That would help keep the population of everything in your woods down to more manageable levels." He looked down at the giant razorback once more.

Dexter took one step back off the tire. He seemed to glide back to the ground in slow motion. "Don't worry about the cost of roasting, Henry. I'm sure we can work something out later."

Cheryl turned to Ansel whispering, "We need to be more business savvy like them." Ansel sighed. He only nodded at his sister. He had thought similar things over the last few years watching Dexter steadily build the werewolves' wealth. They both were a little in awe of the wealth the werewolves had accumulated in such a short period of time.

Now he saw how quickly Dexter moved to make things happen and vowed to do the same for his shifters. The shifters he governed were vastly different than this tight familial group. One day soon he would have to approach Dexter to see if the uncanny wolf would turn some of his business acumen toward his own group of disparate shifters.

Cheryl like all the others assembled went right up to the open tailgate dragging Ansel right behind her. As he got closer, his chest seized again at the sight of those giant tusks anywhere near Imani's delicate caramel skin. He wanted to shift and claw the dead beast himself.

Chapter Ten

Fireworks

For the first time since she had purchased the car three years previously; Imani rode as a passenger in her own vehicle. The excess adrenaline from her six shifts from human to elephant to War Elephant and back, and the excitement of the actual kill itself were finally leaving her system, but it had given her the shakes. She was too bad off to drive. Henrietta had requested her keys, then forced her nephew Victor to drive Imani to the Lodge. He sat sullenly behind the wheel of her burnt orange Nissan 350z. Henrietta had already warned him in a voice that commanded no resistance, not to go over the speed limit.

"Why did you try to attack me this morning?" Imani asked when they first got in the car.

Seventeen minutes had passed since the question and still Victor hadn't bothered to reply. If Imani hadn't heard him speak this morning; she would have suspected that his jaw might have been wired shut or he was a deaf mute.

As he smoothly braked for a yellow light, Victor finally answered, "You smell different."

"I smell bad?"

"No, not bad. You smell pretty good like peonies and macadamia nuts and sandalwood. It's like I smelled you and I knew everything would change. You smell like change." He turned his head. His espresso colored eyes boring into hers, while his stubborn chin jutted out. "I assumed that Aunt Henrietta was going to force me to marry you. The Herd spent all week talking about you. How pretty you are. How big your family's Herd is. How wealthy your Herd is."

Imani threw her head back and howled with laughter. Tears sprang to her eyes and started leaking down her face. She laughed so long and hard that for a few moments no sound came out.

"Dude!" she finally said leaning all the way back against her headrest and turning to look at him. "The VERY last thing I want to do is marry you. I left my home in Atlanta, so my mother and grandmother and the rest of the Herd wouldn't force me to marry some random bull elephant that I don't know."

Victor looked like she had slapped him. She knew she had wounded him. He turned back to facing the highway as the light turned green. Leagues of pine, white oak and red oak trees lined the highway and Victor put his foot on the accelerator they begun to blur by her car's window. The forest where the Herd communed was north of the city. The Wolf Lodge was south and east of Marshall.

Imani went in for the kill. "Besides, even if your aunt had those ambitions of bringing our Herds together through marriage. My mother and grandmother would probably flat out reject it. I'm the granddaughter and Heir of The War Elephant. Herds from all over the world have been sending their best bulls to try and woo me, court me, kidnap me or even fight me to win me since I started my menstrual cycle and my fourth form emerged."

Up until a few months ago she had been allowed to laugh in the faces of those single bulls and loudly declare she wasn't ready for marriage; but Imani kept the rest of her thoughts to herself. Victor nor anyone else didn't need to know how hurt she had been when her family begin to start pushing her to consider those bulls seriously instead of quickly pushing them out the door on their way.

She scoffed softly, "To be perfectly honest, your Herd doesn't have enough people, clout or money to satisfy my people who are basically Expansionist. My future marriage will be expected to at least double our Herd numbers."

She saw a muscle twitch along his jawline. He didn't like anything she was saying, but deep down he knew she was correct.

Female elephants especially Alphas were expected to marry for the betterment of the Herd. Male elephants were the bargaining chips that helped Herds form alliances, even though their birth herd was given a groom price to compensate the family for the loss of a son. If a herd was small like the Marshall Herd, it would be easier for that herd to intermarry with another smaller herd than to leap up by marrying into a larger herd.

The driveway for Wolf Lodge came quickly. Probably because Victor was flooring her Z up to ninety-five miles per hour. She didn't worry too much. His shifter reflexes should be able to control the car. A sudden thought occurred to her. "You have your eye on someone special, don't you, Victor?" Imani begin to pepper him with questions like the worst little sister ever. "Who is she? What Herd is she from? When did you meet her? Have you told Henrietta that you like her? Has she started negotiations? Do you have your groom price ready?"

That muscle along Victor's jawline ticked again. He stayed silent as they pulled into the parking lot of the Wolf Lodge. Turning the car off, he passed the keys back to her. Opened the driver's door, closed it gently behind him then disappeared around the side of the Lodge.

Imani sighed. She exacted some type of revenge on Victor. She hit him where it hurt the most: his ego. It didn't feel as good as she had hoped.

Gathering herself, she launched herself from the passenger side. Her 'phant scented her kill in the same direction that Victor strode. She followed behind.

There was a great crowd gathered of at least a dozen types of shifters. The metallic tang of blood and fresh meat tinged the air. Imani could scent the types of shifters present but couldn't identify who was who because the scent of razorback and fire were permeating the air. Because of her extended period of shakes from the adrenaline and Henrietta's warning to Victor to drive the speed limit; most of the Marshall Herd had beat her and Victor here.

Everyone was watching a dozen werewolves who were scrambling around busily skinning the massive razorback which had been unloaded from the back of the truck. On the ground the huge razorback was like a black furred mountain. Silver knives carving the air as they worked seamlessly; operating in one accord the way only a pack could. Another few wolves were building a massive fire in a sunken fire pit.

Four men stood clustered with Coach Henry near the tailgate of his truck. The small group stood a little off from the rest of the crowd of watchers and workers.

"Here she comes, Miss Shifter America!" Henry bellowed across the clearing drawing laughter from the many shifters assembled. "Bull and the wolves are wondering if you want the head and the hide? Otherwise, we can give it to Ada to make hogshead cheese or something else."

"What would I do with the head?" Imani asked curiously. Walking toward the smaller group, she was slightly wary of the large group who lined the perimeter of the private area.

"Have it stuffed and mounted as a trophy?" Henry suggested.

Imani tilted her own head considering. "I wouldn't want to see that thing in my living room. It's going to live in my nightmares long enough," she declared. "Give it to Ms. Ada as thanks for her kindness and feeding me the other night."

"Ada's whole life is about feeding people, she won't accept thanks for what she considers her calling," a man answered. "I'm her husband, Bull."

"Forgive, my manners. Imani this is Bull Harrison, Dexter Waycross, Ansel Junaid and Lester Gains," Coach Henry rushed through. "This is Imani Wilson, she is the granddaughter of Seraphine, the War Elephant."

"I was introduced to Imani at the Alpha meeting earlier this week," Dexter explained to Henry, "but it a pleasure to make your acquaintance again, Imani." He came close. Too close, stepping boldly into her zone of personal space, but he only grabbed her hand and kissed the back of it.

Imani felt a sudden flair of Alpha powers. Strong and potent powers with a metallic ozone twang to them. She felt her elephant perk up again. The 'phant had quieted down to nothing; satisfied from trunk to tail with herself after killing that razorback, protecting the calf and shaming Victor. She had felt a fraction of that same metallic ozone power during at the Alpha Council meeting weeks ago. She looked Dexter in the eyes but felt not even a spark of power from him.

Those powers, the scintillating smell, the homey taste, the warm feel of them against her skin like a crackling fire stirred a familiar feeling of home, acceptance and unconditional love. Those powers stirred zips and zings throughout her body.

Ansel inserted himself between Dexter and her and she felt the source of the metallic and ozone powers coming from him in waves. He grabbed her in a tight hug. "I was worried about you. Henry said you were unharmed, but I needed to see for myself," he whispered in her ear. His deep voice walked ghostly tingles down her spine and into other sensitive places at the core of her.

She felt her elephant screaming inside. The type of screaming that usually prefaced the 'phant trying to rampage all over someone or something. Clamping down on her control, Imani struggled to maintain the elephant on the inside. Her fists balled up so tightly that she could feel her fingernails drawing blood from her palms. The elephant would have nothing to do with Imani's control. Imani was staggered, physically and emotionally by the amount of control she needed to assert to maintain control. Her knees were buckling. Even with her iron fisted control holding, her powers it began to leak out. With one last enormous push back against Imani, the elephant was breaking down all of Imani's shields, her walls brick by brick until they shattered on the floor of Imani's mind. Her control was annihilated by the war elephant in that one moment.

Again, Imani tried a different tactic to soothe her, but she couldn't be comforted or contained and without warning her 'phant released her Alpha powers outwards.

Time slowed as her Alpha powers collided with Ansel's Alpha powers putting on a full color pyrotechnic light show for the whole assemblage to witness. Instantly her 'phant stopped rampaging inside her. The traitorous heifer trumpeted her triumph. Imani couldn't believe what was happening around her. The War Elephant had allowed herself to be claimed. Mated to a stranger.

"Well hello, Miraculous Mate," Ansel said smiling down at her. His white teeth blazing against his midnight dark skin. He pulled her closer. The breadth of his chest as he held her gently making her feel small and petite. "I knew you were going to be trouble the first time I saw you in line for coffee."

"I don't want to mate," Imani stammered out. "Let me go."

"Well the animal inside of you and the animal inside of me say otherwise or it wouldn't have looked like a world class, Fourth of July fireworks show out here a moment ago." His hands lowered from her shoulders to her waist, but the strength of Ansel's hold didn't lessen at all. In fact, it felt tighter. "I'll never let you go, beautiful baby girl, but I won't pressure you for anything quick."

She felt herself blush from hairline to waist where his long fingers gripped her.

He bent down and nuzzled her neck with his nose, inhaling her scent. "You smell like my favorite cookie. I should just nibble here." He trailed his nose up to just behind her ear. "And here." His thick lips leaving a trail of molten fire on the skin below them.

Imani felt her knees weaken and desire flare like a Roman candle inside her.

"Antsy," some woman tugged on Ansel's arm, "why don't we get you two inside before the mating frenzy takes you out here or a brawl happens or..."

"Unhand him NOW!" Imani hissed at the dark-skinned woman. Her angry 'phant rising to the surface trying to force a shift so she could gore a second victim.

"Whoa, Pretty Peony, that's my sister, Cheryl. She isn't a threat. I promise," Ansel declared softly.

Mortified, Imani stammered an apology to Cheryl. Her rage disappeared, but her 'phant was still too close to the surface. She felt her prowling under the skin trying to force her to nuzzle Ansel back or run her hands over his broad shoulders and down to his narrow waist or over the curve of his backside. The 'phant wanted to explore her mate's body until every inch of skin was known to them.

Imani would have to fight both her 'phant instincts and Ansel's somehow. She balled her hands into fists by her side. "I'm so sorry, I don't know what came over me." She couldn't turn to look at Cheryl fully because she was still fully encased in Ansel's arms. Her body was still flush against his from breastbone to knees. She could feel every hard muscle of his body and one muscle in particular was nestled at the junction of her thighs. She stood as still as she could and tried her best to resist the urge to rub herself all over Ansel. She wanted to rip his clothes off and run her hands over all of him. Then rub her body all over him. She wanted to touch him and him to touch her everywhere from her hair line to ankles.

"Mating frenzy," Cheryl and Ansel said at the same time.

"Elephants don't have mating frenzies."

"Your elephant doesn't, but my animal does. It's through our mating bond that you are feeling this way," he said pulling her tighter then rubbing his long nose along her jawline.

"Antsy, please go inside now. Remember the other ladies?" Cheryl prompted.

"Shit." Ansel finally released Imani from his tight hug. Grabbing her hand, he pulled her after him toward the Lodge. "I have a suite here and I would prefer our first time to at least be in a bed because I can't be sure that I'll be a civilized gentleman not when the mating frenzy hits me full force. I've never had a mate before so I'm not sure how to behave." He kissed her knuckles gently, but kept his long-legged stride hurried.

Imani had to hop a couple of times to keep up or she would be pulled behind.

"I have all these conflicting urges," he went on. "Hold you in my arms, take you upstairs and make you scream my name, lick you, feed you, bathe you, shower you with presents, wash you, so many things and that's just my plans for the next hour. I'll make the rest of our lives amazing," he promised solemnly.

She stopped. Putting her whole weight into pulling back against him pulling her forward. As strong as Imani was from years of weightlifting and cross fit and her own natural elephant shifter strength, Ansel was stronger. She was being dragged. "Ansel, I don't want to be your mate. I don't want this."

"Our animals chose one another." He kept walking. They reached the steps. He started climbing, clutching Imani's hand like a lifeline.

Imani grabbed the stair railing with her free hand. Holding tight trying to stop Ansel from dragging her. "I didn't choose this. Are you going to force me?" she asked.

He turned back to her. His expression was more horrified than she felt. "I would never force you. We chose one another."

"No," Imani spit out. "The animals chose. I had no say, but here you are dragging me across the yard with actual drag marks behind us." She refused to let go of the railing and he still held her other hand, but she gestured with her head behind them.

He let go of her hand instantly. He sighed. "I'm sorry. All I can think about it getting you naked beneath me."

"Do you not trust your animal, Imani?"

Imani's world narrowed down to the space where she and the elephant shared a soul. She could feel the elephant pleading with her to accept this decision. The phant knew that every decision that she had made in the last twenty-eight years often lead to a very human Imani suffering the consequences. In short, Imani hated every decision the phant had ever made. Every single one. If Imani had, non-negotiable, HAD to have a mate, she wanted one of her choosing. Not one her elephant, her family, her Herd or anyone else chose for her. She gathered the innate magic of the War Elephant to sever whatever bond was forming between them.

Cheryl came running up. "They're fighting each other now. The wolves are trying to hold them apart, but it won't be long before they come for you two." She flapped her long slender arms in the direction of the door. "Get inside quickly."

He looked back the way they came. He saw a black bear, a lion, a cheetah, several wolves and a couple of large birds of prey fighting. "Please come inside with me, Imani. It isn't safe for you until they are all gone or have fought it out. We will only talk. I promise," Ansel pleaded.

Imani turned her head back to the pit area. She smelled a melee of jealousy, freshly spilled blood, pent up anger and aggression being released. The screeches of bird of prey, combined with the earthly growls of a bear and a dozen wolves filled the air. Reluctantly, she followed Ansel inside.

"Elevator or stairs?" he asked.

Thoughts of being in a tight space alone with Ansel when she could still feel tingles from the weight of his hands on her body earlier... "Stairs."

They jogged up the seven flights of stairs side by side. Ansel led the way to the end of the hall. Two men stood waiting in front of the door to his suite.

"Ansel Junaid, Alpha of the Rare and Unknowns?" asked the man on the left. He was of medium height maybe six feet tall. Slender to the point of an unhealthy, emaciated thin with a skim milk pale complexion, piercing gray eyes and long white blond hair pulled back into a ponytail. The man on the right was shorter and stockier, on the short side five feet seven inches tall. He was a cross between Native American and Mexican heritage with dusky skin, a wide face and strong square jaw, a nose that looked like a Rorschach test from being broken a few too many times with short spiky black hair all over his head connecting into a full beard and razor thin mustache.

Imani turned to Ansel. "Alpha of the Rare and Unknowns?"

He smiled that brilliant knee weakening smile at her as he reached for her hand, intertwining his long fingers with hers. "We've only been mated a few minutes. I was going to tell you probably after I found out your middle name and birth date. Which are?"

"Seraphine after my grandmother and January 9th. You?"

"Come on, you could guess mine. There is really only one famous Ansel..." He trailed a finger down her jaw, titling her head up to look into his onyx eyes. She could see the desire swirling there waiting for them to be alone.

"Ansel Adams the photographer?" Imani stammered out. Ansel's eyes were infinite pools of lust and desire. She was being sucked into the vortex.

"Sir, I'm Special Agent Harrellson," the blond on the left interrupted. "This is Special Agent Orozco. We're with the Stewards. We have intelligence that your impundulu may be in danger. We want to take you into a magical seclusion until the threat is neutralized."

"Sorry guys, our animals just recognized each other as mates. I'm not going anywhere and I'm especially not going anywhere without Imani."

"Impundulu?" Imani asked.

He sighed. Wrapping his free hand around their clutched ones. "Pretty Peony, that's a little more complicated than my Alpha status."

"Felicitations on your mating. We can teleport both you and your mate to our closest safe house." Special Agent Orozco remarked with no inflection in his voice.

"That won't work for two reasons," Imani informed the Agents. "First, I'm not going into magical seclusion or whatever. Second, I'm rubber you're glue whatever magical thing you throw at me bounces off me and sticks right back to you," she warned.

A wicked gleam appeared in Harrellson's eyes. "Imani Wilson? Granddaughter of The War Elephant?"

She nodded curtly.

Both Special Agents bowed to her. "Princess."

It was Ansel's turn to be surprised. "Princess, you're a princess?" he inquired shocked.

"Yeah, informally." Shuffling her feet, she looked down. Those black pools were too much temptation to stare into for too long.

"I didn't know elephants had royal families."

"We don't technically. It's complicated," she mumbled trying to explain and not explain at the same time.

"It is imperative that we protect you Alpha. We have to get you out of here now Alphas," Harrellson interjected.

"I'm not leaving without Imani," Ansel said adamantly.

"I'm not leaving," Imani declared. She felt her latent anxiety flare to life. Mated was bad enough. Unknown danger was a new level of no. She didn't need this type of stress. Never in her life had she wanted to call her mother and grandmother more, even that time Karen Kirkendahl had poured an Orange Julius on the crotch of her all white short set on the seventh grade class field trip to Six Flags over Georgia.

"You leave us no choice," Harrellson said frustrated. Both shifters felt his temper flair disproportionately to the situation. "We're invoking the Alpha Protection Act." Referring to the arcane law that allowed Steward Agents the power to override an Alpha's final word and use magic to force an Alpha to comply for the 'greater good' or against their better judgement. Alphas especially with the followers were their own final authority. It was even written into law, Section One, Subsection One of the Shifter Civil Rights and Autonomy Act of 1968.

Ansel looked at Imani with remorse in his eyes as Harrellson and Orozco started chanting a spell right there in the hallway of the Lodge.

Imani leaned into Ansel's shoulder. "Keep your eyes closed, head down and your back to them," she warned him as she felt the winds of the teleportation spell begin to invade the hallway. "This is going to get nasty." Jerking Ansel's hand, she forced him down onto the carpeted floor to kneel next to her. She took a deep breath, inhaling his scent as he had done her earlier. Inside she erupted, her body quavered with like a magnitude seven on the Richter scale. Ansel smelled like an icehouse, a cool spring day after the rain and a summer barbeque. The smell of him was divine. His scent sent waves of desire flaring through her body. More and more, she just wanted to give in and strip naked and let Ansel have his way with her.

He wrapped his arm around her waist, pulling her closer as if he was protecting her and not the other way around. Everywhere he touched her left a trail of fire on her skin and in her blood.

The Agents spoke the final word of the spell. The howl of the winds stopped, silence reigned. Harrellson looked at Orozco. "We should be in Houston..." He words were cut off as all the magic they had unleashed came swirling in one enormous, glowing orb of blue and green tinged magic directly toward them. It passed through Harrellson and into Ansel's solid oak suite door behind leaving a path of destruction. A large, jagged hole appeared in the outer wall of the suite like a large pipe bomb had exploded. Harrellson's eyes rolled into the back of his head, showing only the whites. He went limp then collapsing to the floor. Orozco dropping to the floor beside his partner. He started to administer first aid.

Imani stood to her full height. Shaking dust and other debris out of her hair and off her shoulders. "I did warn you two."

"Did you just deflect a spell cast by two Steward Special Agents?" he asked on bended knee.

Imani could hear the awe in his voice. It unexpectedly gave her a little thrill. Normal male shifters ran like their hair was on fire when they learned the full extent of her powers or more precisely that there was no full extent to her powers.

"Tell me," he commanded. His Alpha voice shredding her insides to an oatmeal like mush.

She sighed. "You know that whole Princess thing?"

Ansel nodded as he stood to his full height beside her, never letting go of her hand. "It's tied to the War Elephant title."

"What's the difference between a regular elephant shifter and a War Elephant?" he asked. He was running the fingers of his free hand, down and up and down her arm like his was trying to memorize the texture of her skin. Every pass of his hand touched something deeper than her skin. He was touching the essence of her.

"A War Elephant is a twenty-ton armored beast with an impenetrable hide with three sets of tusks like huge ivory scimitars. She can take out a tank or a squadron of tanks if she wants. Magic just bounces off her hide. If there is a physical threat to any elephant under her protection, she becomes a ruthless killing machine until the threat is eliminated."

She did her best to ignore the feeling of invasion as he continued to rub her, but the elephant was almost preening at their touch.

"Exactly how many War Elephants are there?"

"In history or just right now?"

"We'll start with right now. Later, we'll do the history."

"Okay, right now there are two living War Elephants. My grandmother and me."

Ansel smiled that megawatt smile again. "You get more impressive by the minute, Princess Cookie. Our life is going to be so interesting."

Imani tilted her head placing her hand on her hip at that comment. "I just told you I turned into a twenty-ton elephant of mass destruction and all you have to say is 'interesting'?"

Orozco chose that moment to join their conversation. "Harrellson is alive, just unconscious. Since we can't teleport you out, we will have to find alternative means of transportation." He pulled out a cell phone and begin barking orders as soon as the line was answered.

"How many times do I have to say that I'm not going?" Imani queried.

"Even if I told you my life and my soul were in danger," Ansel asked. He was still holding one of her hands in both of his. The warmth of his body was spreading throughout her own body leaving a driving sexual need in its wake that she had never felt before. "And you might be the only person who could save me?"

Chapter Eleven
Road Trip to Hell

"I thought we were supposed to meet your convoy an hour ago," Imani complained from what was now the backseat of her two-seater convertible car. Orozco had taken one look at her car, cursed, then waived his free hand at her car. His other hand was occupied carrying Harrellson over his shoulder. Her car had shaken and rumbled then bubbled a "backseat" out of the trunk area.

The new backseat was smaller than the front area with no actual seat just the carpeted floor of the car. Ansel had tried to squeeze back here with her, but at six foot seven he didn't fit. Harrellson, since he was the main channel of the teleport spell, was still unconscious. Orozco had carelessly tossed him into the back with Imani as he slid behind the steering wheel.

Three hours sitting with her legs crossed as her preschool cousins called it crisscross applesauce had her cramped and sore. The magically deformed car hit every bump in the road, she was sure to have sustained a concussion from one spectacular Texas-sized pothole that tossed her into the roof.

Orozco was using some type of obfuscation or invisibility spell as they traveled at a speed in which the engine's governor should have turned the car off. Imani couldn't see the speedometer as she sat at a right angle behind the Agent, but she was sure at several points they were doing close to one hundred and fifty miles an hour. From her profile view of Ansel's less than amused face, she could tell she wouldn't be happy at all with the treatment of her baby.

She'd heard numerous pings and several clangs underneath the car. A few times she even felt the tires leave the road as Special Agent Demolition Driver used her prized possession as a demolition derby reject. He hadn't hit anyone directly, but she was sure he had magicked a few cars out of his way using the front bumper like a ram.

At one point after the car had gone airborne then crashed back to the ground with a loud screech, Ansel had turned to her and mouthed, "I'll buy you a new car."

"We keep moving until we are at the safe house," Orozco said through clenched teeth.

The strain on him had to be tremendous. There was no telling how many spells he was using at one time to hide them from whatever was chasing Ansel, the car itself, clearing people out of his way as he maintained such a dangerous speed and keeping the human police from pulling them over. Steward Agents like their human FBI counterparts normally worked in pairs. Sometimes they operated in triads to keep a balance of magic, shifter strength and speed and specialized law enforcement training for this reason.

She looked at Agent Harrellson tucked in the fetal position of what should have been the rear wheel and sighed. Imani was pretty sure she hadn't figured into their plans when they came for Ansel, but she didn't feel bad for either Agent. She had warned them of her magical immunity. They had chosen to ignore her warning.

Of course, she could have explained the magical immunity better, but if they knew enough about her grandmother and Herd life to call her 'princess' then they should have known enough to heed her warning no matter how childishly she said it.

As soon as she got her hands on the Special Agent in Charge, she was going to give him/her/them/it all the pieces of her mind she could.

"It's been three hours and—" she checked her dying phone display, "—twenty-seven minutes. I'm starving. I haven't eaten since last night's dinner. My 'phant was denied eating her kill. She really isn't that possessive and vindictive, but right now she really wants to smash you flat."

"We're almost there. Thirty more minutes."

Imani recognized the tone Orozco used. It was the same one her father used on her during long summer road trips when she would ask from the backseat. 'Are we there yet?' Her father would always answer 'thirty minutes' whether they were ten minutes away or ten hours away.

"I won't make it that long or far. I at the very least need a bathroom now."

The air in the car begin to dry out and smell faintly of ozone. "Agent, pull over. My mate needs relief," Ansel said in a tone that raised all the hairs on Imani's arms.

Imani had heard her father use that tone once defending her mother. It gave her a small thrill that someone would use that same tone in defense of her.

Orozco gripped the wood grain steering wheel tighter. Imani could almost hear it cracking. Orozco explained patiently and calmly, "If I stop all the spells right now, I may not be able to resume them. I just don't have enough power left in my tank, so to speak. If Harrellson was conscious then maybe we could risk it."

"Ansel, I'll try and make it. If not, I'll need new clothes," Imani urged. She didn't want to witness Ansel get angry for the first time in an enclosed space. She was sure he had a good grip on his animal, whatever an impundulu was, but she didn't want to take a chance.

"What is an impundulu?" she asked as she reached out to touch his bare forearm. She had followed his arm movements almost the whole drive. His arms were long and lean; the biceps, triceps and extensor muscles were well defined. He wasn't bulky like a bodybuilder more like a linebacker. She had looked her fill at him and couldn't find any fat anywhere her eyes could see. When the yearning to have his muscular arms wrapped around her again became too much, she planned work out programs for him in her head to distract herself.

Ansel turned his head slightly. He smiled, all his straight white teeth blinding her. "I would love to show you which is easier. I would much prefer our 'getting to know each other' phase wasn't happening as we were flying down I-45 being driven by Special Agent Maniac."

Special Agent Orozco grunted, but otherwise just kept looking forward as they rocketed down the highway.

Ansel reached between the seats offering her his hand. The moment their fingers touched heat flooded her body. His long lean fingers intertwined with hers and she felt her heart lighten. The longer they touched the hotter her body felt and the more sexually turned on she became. The calmer, more centered her heart became too. She had sat next to Harrellson long enough to know he was the Agent with the strong shifter scent and Orozco had no shifter scent that she could detect.

"Are you as turned on as I?" she whispered almost to herself, hoping Ansel's enhanced shifter hearing could make out her words.

"More so. I could hammer nails right now and I'm not talking about with my hands." Imani heard Ansel whisper back. She grasped his hand tighter. "It's taken everything in me to keep from crawling back there with you. My animal wants to claw everything in its path to get to feel you in my arms."

"I've never heard of an impundulu before today."

"You won't. First, there are less than two dozen of us all over the world. We are an endangered species."

"Do you have breeding problems? Because I can tell you now this is going to go badly. When I'm ready for children, I need to have daughters, lots and lots of daughters," Imani said louder than she meant to, going way above the whisper they had been using.

"The impundulu is normally passed to the males of the line. The female children are whatever animal the mother is, there are a couple instance where girl children are both impundulu and another animal, but those are rare." He squeezed her hand. "I'll give you all the baby—" he paused, "What are baby elephants called?"

"Calf, calves," she trailed off.

"I'll give you all the girl calves we can handle."

"It's not me, it'll be the Herd."

"How big is your Herd?"

"My blood related family Herd is about ninety. Our extended Herd is a few hundred. How many are you Alpha of?"

"One point seven million."

Imani froze. Her brain refused to process the number that Ansel had whispered.

"One point seven million people!" she shouted.

Ansel laughed. "Yes, one point seven million shifters. The Rare and Unknowns are all the shifters worldwide who don't have a blood group or in case of a few were kicked out or outcast from their blood group."

"How do you govern that many people?" Imani asked. She had a hard-enough time assisting her mother governing the few hundred elephants in their Herd.

"With help, lots of help. After the War, my father who was the first Alpha of the Rare and Unknowns realized the problem that we once we took in everyone who didn't have a group large enough to make their own clan/herd/pack whatever that we would need a decentralized system to govern. We have a structure similar to the Alpha Council with local, district, regional, national and international groups."

"So, you don't have any daily duties?"

"Quite the opposite, I have a staff of fifteen people in Marshall that help me run our Headquarters. I only teach at Wiley part time because I spend the rest of the day at Headquarters. Let's not talk about duty. I want to know all about you! How did you really end up in Marshall?"

Imani sighed. "I was running away from my duty."

"What duty is that?"

"To become the Herd Broodmare, get married and start a family, have as many daughters as possible, move up my Alpha training," she whispered even lower than the rest of their conversation.

Ansel's low chuckle washed over her prickling gooseflesh down her arms. "You ran away from your matchmaking momma right into my loving arms?" he asked, before she could answer he continued, "Fate can be so cruel. Here I've been hoping with all hope that Fate would be kind and send me a mate just like you before it became too late. You are everything I've ever wished for in a mate — strong, sexy, smart and capable. While I've been wishing for you, you've been trying to run away from Fate. Maybe you weren't running away from your Herd, maybe you were running toward me?"

The driving sexual need which had never gone away from earlier went from a low simmer to a full boil as Ansel continued caressing her fingers. The low whispered exchange was another intimate caress to her heightened senses.

Ansel untangled their fingers, so he could trace his long index finger around her jawline, titling her head upwards toward the roof of the car. His fingers ran feather light from her chin down her neck and even further down to the exposed skin of the tops of her breasts.

"So soft," he murmured. Ansel continued to skim his fingers running feather light over her exposed skin, face, neck, shoulders, and down her arms. His breathing was ragged like he ran a marathon to get to her.

Imani could feel everything in her responding to his touch. Her skin was on fire. Every nerve wanted to leap out of her body for more of his touch. Her breasts were swelling. Her junction moistened. Her clit was painfully swollen from their earlier contact of their bodies and she could feel it grow even larger. Her elephant was trumpeting her desire to be mounted from behind as quickly as possible, to the exclusion of all other sounds. Another intimate caress from those long fingers to her body and she would explode.

Ansel snatched his hand and arm away from her. He grabbed at the steering wheel yelling, "Special Agent!"

"Imani shake him. He's passed out with his foot on the gas."

Imani grabbed the agent and shook him hard. She felt no response from him under her hands. His magic was gone. He was drained.

Her heart slammed into her chest as panic rose. Ansel swerved her Z around a slow-moving minivan and she felt the car tilt onto the shoulder before Ansel corrected.

"Anything?" she asked still shaking the Agent.

"Nothing. He must have drained all of his magic and passed out!" Ansel's voice was calm, but she could hear his heartbeat going just as fast as her own like a runaway freight train.

She jabbed her finger into Ansel's seat belt freeing him. Then jabbed her finger into the Special Agent's buckle releasing him.

"I'll pull him out. You get behind the wheel." She could hear her voice going stringent.

"Okay, on three!" Ansel commanded. She saw him pulling his long legs up off the floor while trying to control the wheel.

"One. Two. Three!" he shouted.

Imani pulled on her 'phant's strength to yank the Special Agent up and out of the driver's seat. The Agent came out of the driver's seat like cold Jell-O. He seemed stuck on something, but she bore down pulling harder and after a moment's tension he slid free.

She pulled him into the 'backseat'. There was barely room for her back there, no way was she going to share with the Special Agents who were supposed to be "protecting" them. She climbed to the passenger seat.

Ansel slowed the car down and moved into the right lane so that they could exit the freeway. Without her asking, he pulled off at the next exit and straight into the gas station rolling to a stop next to a pump.

"You head inside to the ladies' room and I'll fill the tank up. Looks like Special Agent Orozco was magicking the gas tank too. The arrow is below the E." He leaned across the seat kissing her forehead. "After that, we'll grab some lunch. Okay?"

"Sounds like a plan." She was already out the door and power walking across the parking lot.

Imani came back about ten minutes later to find Ansel leaning against the passenger side door scrolling on his phone.

They hugged. Imani wasn't sure whose arms wrapped around who first, but together they just stood there under the gas station awning. They could have stood there minutes or hours. No words were spoken, but no words were necessary. Imani's heart rate which had spiked again during the insanity of the Agent's passing out was now normal again.

He kissed her on the forehead again before opening the passenger door for her to slide in. "I know you didn't get any of your kill this morning, but I can't find a game restaurant nearby. There's a steakhouse twenty minutes away. A bar-be-que place ten minutes away."

Closing the passenger door, he came around to the driver's side continuing his breakdown of the food options. "I'll eat anything. There's some chain restaurants at the next exit up alongside a bunch of fast food places."

Imani paused in buckling her seatbelt. She wanted something that had been slow smoked for hours and falling off the bone. "Bar-be-que sounds good."

"Perfect. Just like you," Ansel said as he pulled up the directions on his phone.

Imani felt a blush rising up her face at those simple words. She turned to look out the window ignoring the response that was on the tip of her tongue. *No, you're the perfect one,* she thought instead.

Before long they were flying down a narrow two-lane country road. Ansel's right hand gripping her left like he was afraid she would float away if he didn't keep hold. Imani wished that they could let the top down, but with the magic that was done to her baby there was no telling what exactly would happen if they tried to let the convertible down.

Twelve minutes later, they pulled up to the bar-be-que restaurant that looked more like a ramshackle outhouse than a five star rated bar-be-que joint. Ansel looked back and forth from his phone to the place. "I think this is the right place. I can't be sure. They don't even have a sign anywhere."

Imani opened her door and the smells hit her in a tsunami of wood smoke. She smelled everything from beef, pork, chicken, baked beans and two dozen other food scents that drove her stomach wild with anticipation. She felt a bit like Homer Simpson as a puddle of drool formed in her mouth.

"It doesn't look like much," Ansel started. A frown marring his features. He got out of the car following her.

"I don't even care what it looks like out here obviously all the work goes into the food," Imani interjected before he could go any further and recommend they leave. "Can't you smell it?"

The porch surrounding the grey weathered clapboard place was made up of unevenly cut boards that weren't nailed all the way down as evidenced by some of the nails being bent into horseshoe shapes.

"Let me carry you," Ansel said taking one look at the crooked porch and bent nails. "You only have those flip flops on and we don't need to have to get a tetanus shot as a side dish."

She ignored his offer to carry her. Walking gingerly across the three-foot wide porch, she dodged nails and open spaces between the porch boards. She reached for the handle of the restaurant's front door. Imani turned the handle and pushed. The door didn't move. She turned the handle and pulled. The door didn't move. She put some of her weight behind the shove and tried again.

Nothing.

Ansel took over pushing and shoving, pulling and pushing for a few moments.

"Most people know to just come around back," a voice called.

They both turned toward the sound.

"This is Pop's Smokehouse BBQ?" Ansel questioned.

Imani turned and hopped off the porch and went in the direction of the guy with the apron tied around his waist and evidence of either a blood bath or according to her nose – a tangy sauce.

"Sure is. I'm Quad." He held out a meaty hand to Ansel first, then Imani. Gripping them both hard enough to the crack small bones in each of their hands. Gesturing to the shack with his free hand. "That door has been nailed shut at least twenty years since Big Pop Junior went to man that big smoker in the sky."

Quad moved slowly and stately. Like a shifter who was once injured very badly and never healed properly. He looked anywhere between thirty and fifty, with a wide face, thick eyebrows and unblemished walnut skin and a large wide nose with nostrils you could drive a car into and park it.

They followed Quad to the back of the shack. A lush garden with a dozen wooden picnic tables greeted them. Each table was covered in a wildly printed tablecloth of check and florals, a caddy with different sauces, a roll of paper towels.

All the tables were empty.

"Are you closed?" Imani queried. Looking around at all the empty tables and empty parking lot, she couldn't understand why the place wasn't packed with all the yummy smells coming from the pit smoker that dominated one side of the garden.

"Nope. This is just the lull between lunch and dinner. In another hour, all the tables will be full, and some people will be camped out on blankets. It's Saturday; around six tonight I'll put up the big screen and show old movies."

Quad moved behind a long quartz counter that was positioned just in front of the giant pit smoker. The closer Imani moved to the twenty-foot long smoker the more her stomach growled.

"What can I get you folks?"

"I'll have a rack of ribs," Imani asserted happily.

"She's from Georgia. She doesn't know what she's doing," Ansel said with a smile, grabbing her hand and kissing it. "Let us get a taste of your sausage, brisket and the ribs. Both the beef and pork."

Quad just smiled. He turned his back to them and pulled several meats off the smoker, slicing thin pieces and pushing them across the quartz to them.

With his meat cleaver, he gestured at each cut. "This is the regular sausage, jalapeno sausage, smoked boudin." Turning back again to the smoker, he pulled out several more.

Several deft strokes later, he offered more samples, "Chicken, brisket, pork rib, beef rib."

He turned again. "Bacon wrapped shrimp, bacon wrapped chicken."

"I can also do you a steak on the pit – ribeye, filet, New York strip, T-bone."

Imani tasted every sample he offered. Her eyes got bigger and bigger the more she tasted. Every bite was juicy and flavorful with spicy, tangy sauce and herbs and seasoning perfectly smoked exploding over her tongue. She must have communicated her indecision to Ansel.

He chuckled lowly as he finished his last sample of bacon wrapped chicken. "I'll take care of this, Princess."

"Give us a half pound each of all three sausages, a slab of pork and slab of beef, half a chicken, a pound of brisket. Do you have potatoes and corn in there?"

"Of course," Quad scoffed. "This is a real Texas BBQ place run by my family for over seventy years." Pride evident in his stance.

"We'll also have two baked potatoes and two corn on the cob and large of each of the sides. What do you have for dessert?"

"My mom's peach cobbler, a blueberry cobbler, and 7Up pound cake," Quad answered proudly.

"Two of those each too. Got to feed my hungry mate," Ansel said rubbing her back in long strokes.

"Aww, mates. That explains it. Spent all day burning calories." He laughed with a suggestive waggle of his thick eyebrows. He went back to slicing with those sure strokes. Sliding two flat plastic trays topped with wax paper and loaded to the breaking point with meat goodness down the quartz counter. Quad grabbed Styrofoam containers and began stuffing them full of macaroni and cheese, baked beans, coleslaw, green beans, and potato salad.

"Brother, I wish that's how we spent the day. You have no idea how hard she is fighting me and the whole mate thing."

"Our animals just recognized each other like five hours ago, if that long," Imani said with a bite to her tone.

"She wouldn't be worth it if she didn't put up a fight or you have to fight for her," Quad said, staring deep into Ansel's eyes. He looked like he wanted to say more, but at the last moment changed his mind.

Imani wondered at Quad's hesitation but shrugged it off. He stuck forks in each Styrofoam container on a third flat tray and slapping stacks of thick sliced bread down alongside everything else including the desserts.

They arrived at the register. Quad's hand flew over the touch screen adding up their huge order.

"I sell cokes by the can, water by the bottle, lemonade and sweet tea by the half gallon and whole gallon.

"Give us a whole gallon of sweet tea."

Ansel handed Imani the lightest tray and told her to go find them a table. He and Quad finished with the bill while she picked a table with the least garish of the loud garish tablecloths on the far side of the clearing, near the wood line of the forest. Ansel followed, carrying the two heavier trays. He sat on the same side of the bench as her, sliding his long legs into the bench seat. Sliding down, he sat close enough for their thighs to touch from hip to knee.

Quad followed carrying a gallon of dark brown sweet tea with his own label 'Pop's Smokehouse' on the front and two huge Styrofoam cups of ice.

"Aren't you sitting kind of close?" Imani asked reaching for slices of Texas toast.

"Pretty Peony, if we weren't in public, I'd have you naked in my lap while I fed you tiny morsels of food, so you never got full and I could keep you there longer."

Imani gave him a narrow-eyed glare and asked, "You do realize elephants gore people?"

Ansel's hand paused mid-air as he was reaching for something in the center of the table.

Quad burst out laughing. "Bruh, I wish you all the luck with this one. She might be more than you can handle," Quad said as he placed his burden on the table. "I'll leave you to your courting." The he went back to the long quartz counter.

Chapter Twelve

Escape

Her cell phone hissed against the glass desktop. She loathed the smartphone and wished people just went back to communicating through crystal balls again. She wiped the screen. "I marked him over water like you instructed."

"Good."

"There's something else. Right after I marked him, he mated with some other shifter. I started a fight with the other women hoping that I could get away in the confusion. Maybe get to him and kidnap him or something." She paused. "Before, I could sneak out of they had disappeared from the Lodge and everyone is looking for them. His suite was trashed magically, but no vehicles are missing. Since he's missing, their asking us to wait to speak with the Stewards. Then we 'are free to leave' the sister told us. I might not get another opportunity to see him much less be alone with him."

A red tipped black nail reached out and pressed 'End'.

A scream with decades of frustration rent the air.

Chapter Thirteen

The Reveal

"I think he might be right," leaning in close, Ansel whispered to her. "You might be more than I can handle." The impundulu could feel her reluctance, her resistance, her fighting the mating bond. It felt like perforated paper right when enough pressure was applied, and the full sheet was being torn out of the book. A steady pressure from her and it would rip. Severing them apart. That was the very last thing he wanted. He couldn't imagine his life without her. The mating frenzy was making him insane. If she left, he would be insane, and Cheryl would have to assume the Alpha role.

She blushed.

Every time she blushed his heart skipped a beat. He was thankful for the low-cut tank-top, so he could watch it spread over her face and body the way he wished it was his hands or mouth.

Ansel was eighty percent certain that she didn't have on a bra and panties. He was going to make it one hundred percent certain as soon as she finished eating. The nearest hotel was sixteen miles away due west and he had booked a room while filling up the car. Luckily, whatever blocking spell the Steward agent had used on their phones while in the car stopped the minute he got out of the car.

Unfortunately, his phone was on two percent and dying fast while Imani's was already dead.

"Imani, no matter what, I want to be everything you need, deserve and desire. If I fail at something, just tell me and I'll never make that mistake again," he admitted sincerely.

Her blush deepened and the scent of her arousal, which had been the main scent in his nostrils since their animals recognized each other at the Wolf Lodge spiked to a new high. Her arousal was driving him insane. She smelled like a fresh batch of white chocolate and macadamia nut cookies straight out of the oven. Ansel didn't care if it would scorch the skin off his face, he wanted to bury his nose into the junction of her thighs. He spent several long moments talking himself and the impundulu out of grabbing her and carrying her off into the forest so he could unveil her body to his eyes and hands and most assuredly his mouth.

They could make it to the hotel.

They could make it to the hotel.

They could make it to the hotel.

They could make it to the hotel.

He repeated this mantra in his head to the impundulu who he felt bristling against waiting a second longer.

They had to make it to the hotel.

She deserved for their first time to be special, not a quickie in the woods. Making love to their mate in the woods would have to come later.

Instead of following the impundulu's instincts for mating now, he passed her the bottle of Quad's sweet, spicy and tangy sauce as she built a towering sandwich with two kinds of sausage, half the container of coleslaw and three pieces of bread.

She squirted sauce everywhere inside the sandwich. Then bit into it with gusto. She moaned as she chewed. Imani was not going to be too embarrassed to eat in front of him and he was so proud. He considered himself a foodie, both in cooking and in dining out. His credit cards and airline statements were a reflection of his love for restaurants near and far.

There was nothing more he loved than to watch people eat. Especially if they were enjoying food the way Imani was currently doing as if this was her last meal.

The next fifteen minutes the air was punctuated with chewing sounds and the little noises of happiness Imani made when she sank her teeth into an especially tasty bite of food.

Imani set the rib bone down that she had cleaned and jerked in and out of her mouth in one smooth motion stripping all the meat from the bone. He became even more turned on watching her eat. Every time, he thought he had mastered his control of his ever-hardening erection; Imani again made some new sound or gesture with her mouth testing all of his control not to snatch her up from the table and carry her into the woods surrounding Pop's. Years from now, he didn't want to regret not making their first time together special with soft sheets, candles and hours of foreplay.

He didn't want to be one of those mates who barely remembered their first times because they were driven by lust or compelled by the mating frenzy, but the noises she made while eating were just enough to drive him over the edge of his barely held control.

She licked her lips, then grabbed a paper towel to wipe her mouth and fingertips. He opened his mouth to offer to lick her clean, but a family of six with very young little ones came around the corner. Ansel instead bit into a large piece of chicken.

"I want to know why your soul is in danger," she asked without preamble.

The juicy bite of smoked chicken turned to ashes in his mouth. He struggled to finish chewing and swallow the last bite. "Can't we start with something easy? Like why all elephants in a family have names that start with the same first letter? Henrietta. Henry. Harriett. Victor. Veronica. Vlad."

She sighed, ignoring his question and stalling tactic. "Ansel, I'm here because of this bond. I actually can feel the bond growing stronger the longer we are together. I never expected to have a destined mate. Elephants don't marry for love, we marry for power and position and for the good of the Herd."

Imani had been looking down at her hands in her lap as she spoke. She looked over at him and placed one hand on her heart and her other hand over his heart. "This bond between us is incredible. It's like a string between your heart and mine. The closer we are to each other the thicker it gets. If I didn't feel this bond between us strengthening and growing by the minute, I wouldn't be here. Otherwise, I would have stayed at home. Don't leave me in the dark." Their bond pulsed at her words.

Ansel sighed deeply. "You want the long version or the short version?" He grabbed one of the premoistened paper towels off the rolls to clean his face and hands.

"Long."

Closing his eyes briefly, he began, "About one hundred and thirty years ago, a newly mated Maasi couple was kidnapped and enslaved by what they would today call a super coven of magic users. Dark magic users. They tortured the couple with spells both mentally and physically. The torture lasted until they were just shells of people and their animals."

He paused as he watched Imani's eyes grow wide and her hands flew to her mouth. Without asking, he grabbed her hands – holding them in one of his.

"Then they used the couple as spies against their enemies. Assassins occasionally."

He took a deep breath and continued, "After about three years, one of the witches, wizards, voodoo priests, a coven member – had the brilliant idea that they needed more slaves like this mated pair. First, they tried to find more mated couples. The process didn't work on the next dozen couples quite so well. Eventually they ended up killing thirty couples trying to magically enslave them like that first couple."

"Instead of giving up, they just focused on the same type of shifters that the mated pair were – impundulus or as we are referred to in fables — lightning birds. They decimated a whole tribe of lightning bird shifters looking to find a newly mated pair who would be susceptible to the magic and spells like the first couple had."

He grabbed a paper towel and wiped the tears streaming down Imani's face. "It's okay, Cookie, there will be a happy ending eventually."

She blinked at him but didn't respond. He could see the shimmer of more unshed tears gathering in her eyes.

"It took about five years before they gave up hunting lightning bird shifters. Most of the impundulu by that time had been killed, those who were alive fled the entire continent of Africa for parts unknown. They went back to the couple and inundated them with fertility spells. Forcing them to mate continuously, in three years they had four children. Two boys and two girls, unfortunately for the magicians the girl children were immune to most of their spells. The boys however were more susceptible to their spells. Turns out unmated and newly mated male lightning birds are very susceptible to magical influence. Skip forward a decade, the male of the couple was injured while trying to assassinate one of the coven's rival magic workers."

Grabbing both of her hands into one of his, he continued, "The witch he attempted to assassinate was very old and pretty powerful. Instead of just killing the impundulu she captured him, holding him until she undid all the magic she felt holding him enslaved. She eventually broke the spells that was holding him captive which through the mating bond freed the wife. The wife was able to escape with both daughters and one of the sons. They tried to rescue the remaining son, but it was too late. He was fully enslaved. The couple, Laibon and Naserian, like the rest of the impundulu, felt they had no choice but to leave the entire continent of Africa and go on the run. They travelled the world – India, Australia, South America then eventually North America. For twenty years afraid to settle anywhere while raising their children and trying to forget their captivity. Laibon and Naserian were my grandparents."

By this time, Imani was heaving in great sobs of air and tears. She still cried just as quietly as before but her whole body was engaged. Chest heaving, eyes leaking, foot tapping the ground like she was trying to expel the emotional pain with a physical act.

"Cookie, please stop crying."

"I can't. That is too depressing and tragic to contemplate. Did they have this bond we share? If something happened to you would I feel it?" More tears streamed from her eyes and she started sobbing uncontrollably.

Ansel gathered her up in his arms and carried her seventy-five yards into the woods. Finding the sturdiest tree, he sat at the base with his mate on his lap and let her cry herself out. He rubbed her back with long strokes and whispered nonsense in her ear.

"Imani, please stop crying," he pleaded.

Imani paused for a moment — mid sob. "Did you just call me by my name?"

"Well yeah, I was starting to get worried." Ansel turned her face to his. "That didn't seem like a normal cry."

"I don't think it is either. Not sure why or how, but everything just kind of exploded out."

"You have, or should I say we have been through a lot today. You had to kill a razorback to defend a child. I had to fight off a half dozen, greedy, money hungry, marriage minded women. Then we mated and got swept away by shifter law enforcement. Any of those things would make for an eventful day, but we had them all today."

"I don't even think it has been just today. This has been a wild upside-down kind of month for me with the move and everything."

"I'll make it all better, Princess Cookie. I promise. We'll find a new normal together."

"There you go again with the nicknames. I like the sound of your voice saying my name. Just hearing you say it at the Alpha Council kept me distracted most of the night," she admitted. "Your voice is very deep and sexy."

Ansel smiled at her admission, wrapping his arms around her in a tight hug. "Wait until I get you in a bed between some soft sheets, I plan on whispering to you all types of dirty sexy things."

Imani blushed then realized where she was sitting or more pointedly what she was sitting on. Ansel was rock hard beneath her. She exhaled, and her body went back to fully turned on.

"How are you doing this to me?" she whispered, overwhelmed at her body's lightning response to Ansel's body and nearness.

"It's even worse for me," Ansel proclaimed. "I scent even a little bit of your arousal and it takes everything in me not to try to strip you naked and taste you. I've spent all day alternating wanting to grab you and trying not to grab you. It's like there is a fire in my blood and the only thing that will put it out is burying myself into your body and having you scream my name as you orgasm."

"Mating frenzy is amazing." She breathed. She felt their heartbeats sync as they sat quietly for a moment.

"It is. Why don't elephant have them?"

"Not sure, maybe we're too deliberate?" She shrugged.

"Most bird species have them, probably something to do with that's how most bird species mate in the wild – furiously almost savagely. A lot of the time it's even airborne. Some birds and even a few bird shifters result to raping their mates the first time. My kind isn't one of them, butut for some if it isn't going fast enough or sometimes the female is reluctant. They try to push it. A lot of bird shifters have to mate in a certain amount of time, or they lose the momentum, breaking the newly formed bond." He paused, grabbing her hands intertwining their fingers.

"The momentum of the frenzy is said to predict your relationship. We are going to burn long and hard and it is going to be for a lifetime. I can feel it."

"What else should I know about an impundulu?" Imani tried to change the conversation.

"We're out here in the woods. I can show you."

He stood with Imani still in his arms. He felt through the bond that she was mightily impressed with the strength of his arms and core muscles. Ansel just deadlifted her from the ground without any obvious signs of strain. He set her feet on the ground and begin unbuttoning his grey and yellow shirt, while kicking out of his boat shoes. He handed her the shirt and reached for the button of his khaki shorts. Imani averted her eyes. The mating bond between them pulsed with untapped desire. She folded the shirt into a neat square.

He took his shirt from her, then added his shorts and boxer briefs on a nearby stump. He chuckled. A deep sexy chuckle and he watched her body jerk toward the sound.

"Are you going to watch me change, Cookie?"

She turned around and all of his deep midnight skin was on full display for about ten seconds before he started smoothly morphing from a man into what he carried in his soul.

His body, crest and tail feathers appeared solid black, but up close every feather was silver tipped. His wingspan had to be thirty-seven feet, feather tip to feather tip. His beak was burnished silver and the size of a Volkswagen Beetle with a slight hook. His eyes were pure obsidian with flecks of white scattered throughout. Looking directly into his eyes was like staring at a photo of space. He was fearsome. She reached out a hand to run over his feathers, but a wing came down stopping her. She stepped back, but he came forward all eighteen feet of his height dwarfing her. He stuck out a wing again this time sliding it between her thighs and lifted her onto his back.

Chapter Fourteen

Mated

"What do you mean Imani is missing?" Jackie screamed at the phone. The speaker phone sat forlornly on the middle of the empty conference table in the Atlanta Herd's corporate office. Nothing else littered the burnished teak surface – no cups, papers or even a pen.

"How can she be missing?"

"She and Ansel Junaid's animal recognized each other as mates here this morning. It was quite a spectacular firework show. Some of the ladies Ansel's mother had invited here to meet him took exception to them being invited here for nothing. They started a melee. It was all a fury of fur and claws, ripped out feathers and beaks. The werewolves worked hard to break it up, but it was still half an hour before everyone had stopped fighting and went back to human. By the time it was all over, they were missing. Ansel's twin sister, Cheryl said she sent them inside the Lodge when the fighting started. Ansel's room looked like multiple bombs had gone off."

"I decided to call the Stewards instead of the local police, then call you and Ansel's mother," Henrietta said frenzied. "They wouldn't have just left, Cheryl said. Their kind have some type of mating frenzy. The only thing that will be on Ansel and his animal's mind will be the bedroom. Maybe, I should call the local police too."

She paused her voice, a whisper with the heavy blanket of guilt forming in her voice. "I feel so guilty. I invited Imani out to Commune with us this morning, then she had to kill a feral razorback that was charging a girl calf. Not even an hour later, she mated out here in front of the entire Marshall wolfpack and our Herd and all these strangers with no family around. Now she's missing."

"No Henrietta, this is my fault for trying to get her to pick an eligible male before she was ready and apparently when she already had a destined mate out there," Josephine said. "Mother and I will head that way as soon as we can catch a flight. Let us know if you hear anything before we board. If you hear anything after, Janet, my Beta will be running the Herd here."

"I'll let you know if I hear anything," Henrietta promised.

Both Alphas disconnected.

Josephine looked around at her seated sisters and her mother and father plus the several dozen family members standing around the conference room. "Mother and I are headed to Marshall. Get your phones out. Find out everything you can about Ansel Junaid and his family. He has our Heir and we need to know who his family and friends are and who his enemies are and everyone in between before we can make any moves."

"We know Ansel," Seraphine said quietly. "He's the Unknown Alpha."

"Imani is mated to the Alpha of the Rare and the Unknowns?" Joseph, Seraphine's husband and father to Josephine exclaimed. "Well hot damn! Look at my grandbaby go!"

"Hush, you old fool. This isn't the time to celebrate her mating with her missing," Seraphine chided her husband. She grabbed his hand as she spoke. Memories of their own turbulent mating sixty years ago welling up to cloud her heart with emotion.

"Well that is one way to bring in fresh blood to the Herd," Janet said, sat upright quickly. The Herd's Beta went to her phone. She began typing furiously. "There's over a million unknowns, right? We could unofficially become the largest Herd on the planet." The political implications of becoming the largest Herd ran through the Beta's mind and across her face at lightning speed.

"I told her to stay away from him," Jasmine said, ignoring her sister Janet and her father. "I knew he was going to be trouble. He has people after him. I could only see people chasing him and darkness."

"Well those people have us after them now," Jackie the Enforcer said menacingly. She braced her hands on the table, leaning forward. "Find out who his enemies are..." Several Herd members on Jackie's Enforcement team jumped, hastily leaving the conference room while texting or dialing.

"You two head to the airport, Irene will have tickets booked for you by the time you get to Hartsfield," Janet told her sister and mother.

Jacqueline paused before leaving the conference. "Irene, until we know happened to Imani, you are now the Herd Heir."

The entire room stopped at Jacqueline's words. The implications that something major had happened to Imani reverberated through the Herd. A grim feeling descended like rain clouds across a sunny sky. The entire mood of the Herd shifted.

Chapter Fifteen

Not So Special Agent

Harrellson woke to a sharp pain searing through his head and a heavy weight across his legs. Before he opened his eyes, he whispered the spell for a fast-acting pain reliever to take effect in his blood stream. He assessed the rest of his body. Nothing felt broken, but he had woken up in similar situations one too many times to rush into whatever danger was awaiting him on the other side of his closed eyes.

Reluctantly, he opened his grey eyes. Nothing above him looked familiar. He searched his memory for the last thing he remembered. Several moments passed as he struggled through the haze of what had to be a magical concussion if not a physical concussion.

His last memory was invoking the Alpha Protection Act with his partner. "Orozco," he remembered suddenly. He struggled to pull his legs from under the heavy weight trapping him. He sat up to use his arms to help push the weight off his legs. His hands found the familiar feel of his partner's jacket. Relaxing slightly, he pushed Orozco off his legs.

A flail of panic went through him as he quickly checked his partner's vital signs. His pulse was strong, but his magic reserve was completely drained. Orozco couldn't light a candle across a room without a lighter and a helper.

What had happened between the Alpha Protection Act and now? Harrellson wondered. Checking his watch, he saw that six hours had passed since their arrival at Werewolf Lodge. He started chanting a reviving spell over his partner.

Pulling his legs from underneath Orozco's dead weight was exhausting and he jarred his head on something hard causing more pain to shoot through his head. His inner owl and body screeched in distress at the onset of more pain. He searched his pocket for his mini first aid kit pulling it out of the bottomless pocket of his jacket he had magicked last year after he and his former partner, Donovan Douglas were ambushed by a pack of Mexican grey wolves near Brownsville with nothing in the way of supplies.

While he waited for the spells to take effect, he checked his own magic levels. They were tolerable and nothing a month of rest wouldn't top up. His eyesight was fuzzy around the edges and nothing would quite come into focus. He went searching in his pocket once again looking for a light. Finally, he pulled a penlight out.

Orozco woke groggily.

"Dude, I'm so glad to see you awake. My fuzzy brain is playing tricks on me because I could swear we are in the trunk of a car."

"We are," Orozco croaked. "The elephant drove this little two-seater and it was the only transport available unless I wanted to steal from the werewolves to get out of there. I wasn't about to have a full werewolf pack chasing us from Marshall to Houston because we stole one of their cars. They probably threw me back here after I passed out trying to get us to Houston."

"Where are we?"

"Last I remember before passing out was about thirty minutes from downtown Houston and an hour from the safe house."

"So, where are they?"

"Well, if this Alpha is like most of shifter kind; he's either feeding his new mate or looking for the closest bed to consummate their mating."

Chapter Sixteen
A Trip through the Clouds

The impundulu effortlessly glided between an upper thermal above a cloud bank and a lower thermal just underneath, skimming the low-lying clouds. He immediately felt his mate's excitement and wonder through their mating bond. She whooped loudly when he spread his wings again and spiraled downward further until they were skimming the treetops. He flapped his wings a few dozen times gaining speed until they were rocketing by trees too fast to count. Imani just laughed more and grabbed his downy feathers holding on tighter, but still somehow seeming to urge him to go faster. His mate was fearless. The wilder and faster he flew over the last fifty miles the more she loved it.

Her laughter bubbled in the air and he felt those effervescent bubbles exploding in his heart. He would fly her around the world tonight just to keep hearing her laughter, but he could feel Ansel restlessly inside trying to get him to turn around and head back to the clearing where they had taken off. He projected images of him slowly undressing their mate until she only wore her human skin. Leading her into a bathroom, under a hot shower watching water cascade and pebble on her skin. Then soaping her lush body with long strokes using a soap that smelled like some tropical fruit or peppermints or jojoba. Scents he knew the impundulu was fond off.

Reluctantly, the impundulu circled back in the direction from which they had begun. The human was correct. They needed to claim their mate as their own and since she didn't have wings they would need to be inside and away from prying eyes.

Chapter Seventeen

The Seer

Kathleen Junaid stood only five feet five inches tall, but she had the commanding presence of her great, great grandfather Shaka Zulu. Every person on the Alpha's security team, towered over her physically, but they collectively cowered in their own skins as Kathleen continued berating them. "I cannot believe the complete and utter gross incompetence of the lot of you. You…" she said pointing at each of the seven in turn. "How could you lose the Alpha of the largest shifter group in the world? Do you know how many shifters are bonded to him? Your only job is to protect him from danger! Your families, your friends are under his protection so if he is in danger then all of us are in danger. Even if he expressly said 'leave me alone' you should NEVER…"

Cheryl Junaid came rushing into one of the private dining room of the Wolf Lodge that Ansel's team had set up as a War Room. "Mother, Imani's family has arrived," she whispered.

Every shifter perked up at the news. The two humans in the room stayed glued to their screen as they continued their work.

Kathleen stopped her pacing mid stride and her rant mid-sentence. "Seraphine is here?" she mouthed to her daughter. She looked down at her now trembling hands.

"Mom, this is not the time for you to fangirl all over Seraphine," Cheryl said impatiently.

Kathleen just huffed back at Cheryl. "She was my childhood hero.

I had Seraphine posters and trading cards and the comic book. Let me have my moment."

"Well that is great to hear that someone actually had all of that crap," Seraphine said acidly from the doorway as she paused, scanning the entire room before entering.

Every person in the room turned to the doorway frozen in place by the commanding voice of the War Elephant. While Kathleen may have mirrored her ancestor, Shaka Zula in some ways, even as a senior citizen, Seraphine was a reincarnated Shaka Zulu in the flesh. At five feet nine, she was never the tallest woman in the room, with rigid, unbreakable posture she still managed to tower over everyone. Her Alpha powers proceeded her into every room, her own personal red-carpet pushing humans, magic wielders and lesser shifters out of the way and even forcing Alphas secure in their own powers to move out of the way or succumb to the pure tsunami of her control.

Every shifter in the room, bowed low and long to Seraphine. She nodded her head, ignoring the deference paid to her. "If you aren't blood related to us or the male, leave."

The carved double doors of the private dining room were forcefully, flung open as everyone tried at once to disappear from Seraphine's sight. In their rush to leave the room, one door was swung, so violently hitting the wall behind and impressing the werewolf relief carved into the knob half an inch deep into the drywall.

Josephine sighed before pulling out two chairs at the closest table. Both the werelephants sat, staring expectantly at Kathleen and Cheryl. Cheryl excused herself to the hallway, ordering for someone to bring drinks and food before closing the door firmly.

"Henrietta said that the Stewards have been called. Did they say anything? Has one arrived yet? Did you ask the werewolves if they could scent anything? Are there any freelance magic wielders here in Marshall? Did you call one to come out?" Josephine asked. Her emotions peppering the air with worry.

"The Stewards said nothing helpful. They said there were Agents in this area, and they would send them out, but they never arrived.

We called back several times and still nothing from them," Cheryl answered.

Seraphine pulled her phone from her pocket when it started to vibrate. Her silver eyebrows rose into her hairline when she viewed the screen. She whispered to Josephine, "It's the Seer."

"Jasmine?"

"No. The Seer," Seraphine enunciated clearly each word. Seraphine's face remained passive, but her eyes sparked with fear, excitement and worry.

Fear instantly crossed Josephine's face. Kathleen gasped, covering her mouth with her hands. Cheryl looked confused.

The phone continued to vibrate in her hand.

"Mother answer it," Josephine urged.

Angrily, Seraphine swiped the cell phone screen.

"Put me on speaker, Sera," the voice said loudly and clearly. The Seer's heavily Swedish accented voice could be heard clearly without the benefit of the speaker phone but asking to be put on speaker was an indication that the conversation was for all. "Ansel and Imani are alive and bonding well. They left voluntarily with two Stewards; just not the way the Stewards wanted. One of them was foolish enough to attempt to transport Imani with a spell and her magical immunity slapped him hard. He's going to have a spell concussion for six weeks for that." The Seer paused while Kathleen burst into tears.

Josephine sighed and laid her head on her hands, her shoulders rising and falling as she took in deep breathes of air.

"Sera, just because they aren't in danger now doesn't mean they are out of danger. It's why I sent the Stewards to get them in the first place. You must get to the Steward Headquarters Building in Houston before noon tomorrow. I see three futures, all of them converge there. Only one of them has a good outcome."

The call disconnected.

Chapter Eighteen

Flight

Imani braced herself as best she could as she felt the impundulu's muscles move underneath her as he tucked his flight feathers in tight. They were going to land. While she was no longer afraid of falling off the back of the impundulu like she had been during the beginning of their flight, she was now nervous about the landing. She had never experienced flight from the back of an impundulu or any giant bird, but she loved the wind in her face, gliding high in the clouds and skimming the treetops or over a lake. Just the sheer joy of being off the ground, kept her thoughts buoyed.

Her stomach leapt into her throat as they plummeted out of the sky three times as fast as they had been when flying. The impundulu homing in on the clearing near Pop's Smokehouse like a missile.

She couldn't stop her screams from escaping. Flying or in this case falling out of the sky was petrifying and exhilarating at the same time. Just as she was sure that they were going to crash into the clearing below, the impundulu spread his wings fully braking their descent.

Amazingly, they landed gently. Imani slid down the back of the impundulu glad for her feet to be on the ground again. Her hips were tender from straddling the wide back of the impundulu. She watched as the impundulu morphed, blurred and become Ansel.

Ansel nude.

Ansel standing there at full attention, smiling.

The damn mating bond flared between them. She felt his desire for her.

It was overwhelming. Her body heated easily by five degrees. Her nipples hardened.

"I can feel how you want my body," he said smiling even wider than before. He strolled proudly toward the stump where she had folded his clothes before they flew off. He grabbed his shorts first.

She blushed. He was correct. Her eyes tracing one prominent vein from the perfect mushroom tip to root from which it sprang until thankfully his shorts hid her view. Ansel's dick was as thick as her wrist and long as her forearm from wrist to elbow.

She exhaled. She wanted his body badly. Her hands itched to explore every inch of his skin, touching his well, defined muscles and tracing her hands along his eight pack of abdominal muscles and especially his obliques. Her favorite part of the male body. She could picture herself suckling him on the corner of his squared jaw right where his beard ended. Imagined stretching her body out alongside his as they wrapped themselves into what she determined would be a cocoon of ecstasy. Her body bent over the back of a chair as he pounded her from behind with deep strokes that would curl her toes and leave her gasping for air. His mouth grazing the back of her neck with his teeth and small butterfly kisses.

The elephant had her pulling her tank top up and almost over her head. Bed be damned, they could do it right here and right now. The elephant wanted skin on skin contact, and she wanted it now.

"Lucky for you, I want our first time to be in a bed. I want to wash you with my hands, feed you little morsels of food, shampoo your hair, bring you shiny presents."

She had to shut the elephant from her mind completely or she would have stripped them nude and presented herself for mounting like she lived in the wild.

"Shiny presents?"

"It's a bird thing, we love shiny shit." He finished dressing. Covering that wide expanse of smooth midnight skin and sculpted muscles from her sight button by button.

"I don't know a lot of flight shifters. Tell me more," Imani asked as Ansel grabbed her hand and they begin to walk back to Pop's.

Ansel threw his head back guffawing. "I like long flights through the clouds with my mate on my back."

Imani scoffed and playfully punching Ansel on the shoulder. "Be serious, Ansel."

"Well, we have a mating frenzy when we meet our mate," he said turning toward her to wink. "We like to be up high. We always want to be on the top floor of a building. We love gifts – giving especially. Shiny objects attract us to no end."

"Really?" Imani asked disbelievingly.

"Really, shiny things mess with my concentration so much that I can't even have them in my office when I'm working. Everything in my office is matte finished."

"Wow! I never knew flight shifters had such shortcomings."

He stopped, tilting her chin up to his face. "You know what, you are going to be the shiniest thing in my life." He leaned down slanting his mouth over her lush lips. Their kiss sent electric sparks through each of them. Imani could wait no longer, she was the first to push her tongue out and into Ansel's waiting mouth. He groaned while grabbing her neck with his left hand and tilting her head so that he could deepen the kiss. Their tongues intertwined, lapping each other. Imani moaned as Ansel's hand pushed under her shirt. His long fingers of his right hand traced the outline of her firm breast. He kneaded the flesh tenderly before grazing her nipple with his fingertips. The intensity of the kiss deepened when Ansel pulled back from her mouth sucking her bottom lip into his own mouth swirling his tongue over it. He released her lip and dived his tongue back into her mouth. He pinched her nipple this time hard. The pressure shot to her womanhood. Ansel's hand dipped into her sweatpants. His long deft fingers found her junction and he timed his fingers to the rhythm of his tongue.

Imani was lost in a maelstrom of sensations that Ansel orchestrated on her body. It was only a few moments before her body convulsed. Her knees sagged, but Ansel was there to hold her up. Pulling her body flush to his. Deliberately, he pulled his hand out of her sweatpants and sucked the fingers of his hand one by one looking into her eyes. She watched him savor the essence of her on his tongue before he swallowed.

"Best thing I've ever tasted."

He wrapped his arm around her waist. They touched everywhere from ankles to the top of Imani's head. Ansel purred into her ear, "One orgasm down, nine hundred and ninety-nine thousand, nine hundred and ninety-nine to go."

Imani's legs buckled again at his words. She wrapped her arms around his neck. "No way," she whispered into his neck. "I won't survive."

"You'll make it. I refuse to provide less than a million orgasms to my mate. And you definitely are my mate."

She tilted her head back and smiled. "This mate thing might not be so bad after all."

"Come, I need to eat after all that flying and the impundulu wants to feed you little bites of food. Then I reserved a hotel room nearby and I have so many plans for you for later."

"Hopefully, Quad didn't let anyone take our table," Imani said just as they arrived at the clearing. Sitting at their tables and munching on the few leftovers Ansel and Imani had left were Orozco and Harrellson.

Ansel groaned. Ignoring them he went back to the quartz counter to order more food. There was a short line with two people ahead of him, but Quad had a gangly assistant who was slicing with the same long, sure strokes Quad used himself.

Just as Quad had predicted, all the tables were full. Families crowding every available spot, blankets were strewn in the lanes between tables and across the clearing. Everyone was faced toward the back of Pop's shack where Quad had opened a huge screen and was projecting some old animated kids' movie. It was quiet throughout the clearing, most of the little children staring directly at the screen. The smell of hot, buttered popcorn blanketed the air. Imani made her way toward Orozco and Harrellson.

"Glad to see you both awake," she said as she sat down next to Orozco. She reached for the gallon of sweet tea only to discover that it was completely empty. Turning, she caught Ansel's eye, she waved the empty jug at him. He nodded and rolled his eyes, then crossed his eyes.

She chuckled at his antics before turning back to the Special Agents. "I'm surprised that you didn't come searching for us."

"We did," Orozco said pulling a rib out of his mouth. "By air and land, there is no sea around, or we would have searched there."

"Then you should have found us, as we were airborne," Ansel said coming back with another two trays of food and followed by Quad's assistant with a gallon of sweet tea and two cups of ice.

"Cinco, this is my mate, Imani. The one your dad was teasing me about. Cookie, this is Cinco, Quad's son." Placing the two trays vertically in front of Imani, Ansel sat alongside her knee to hip again.

"Nice to meet you, Cinco. What are you going to nickname your son? Seis? Sita?"

"I'm hoping to have all girls just to drive Dad crazy," Cinco said laughingly.

"I think your dad would be happy just for grandchildren," Ansel said.

"Yes, I would be happy for any grandchildren, girl or boy. As long as one of those girls decide that she wants to man or woman the smoker. I'll be happy when I go join the Pops, Senior, Junior and Trey manning the big smoker in the sky," Quad said taking a seat next to Harrellson. He patted the middle of the bench, gesturing toward Cinco. "A sixth generation of our family feeding people good food would make me the proudest."

"Well, that's a good plan ruined," Cinco said, fake pouting.

"I take it, these people are really with you," Quad asked Ansel. Nodding his head in the direction of Orozco and Harrellson. "They came sniffing around maybe fifteen or twenty minutes after y'all hit the woods. I didn't know if they were friends of foes. I put Jimmy and Zeke on high alert."

"Exactly what were Jimmy and Zeke going to do to us?" Orozco asked harshly. He scoffed, "Jimmy and Zeke. Two Texas rednecks in the middle of nowhere."

"Actually, we're Sheriff's Deputies of this county and former Houston SWAT team members," Either Jimmy or Zeke said as they approached the table from behind Quad. Each wore a plaid shirt, frayed jeans and cowboy boots. They also sported military buzzcuts like they were fresh out of basic training, but their eyes held hints of danger. Imani suspected they both had done time in the military serving in wars that didn't have names.

"These are Special Agents Orozco and Harrellson of the Stewards. They're our temporary protection," Ansel said diplomatically. Neither commenting on the friend or foe question that Quad asked.

Imani would have been impressed with Ansel's diplomatic response, but there was more jalapeño sausage and thick slabs of bread. Sandwiches didn't build themselves.

"What did you do to warrant Steward protection?" Jimmy or Zeke asked suspiciously. They still hadn't introduced themselves properly nor did it appear that they would. Their bodies were still on high alert, ready to pounce on someone, anyone. The shifters recognized the coiled readiness. They were spoiling for a fight while everyone else at the table except Quad and Cinco were eating. "Stewards are supposed to inform the local law enforcement, the real police when they are transporting prisoners or witnesses through our jurisdiction."

They glared at both Stewart Special Agents undisguised malice clouding their faces. The differing levels of law enforcement agencies hated one another. Federal hated State, State hated Local and vice versa in a trifecta of interagency jurisdictional enmity. Nothing could unite those three warring factions faster than the appearance of one lone Steward Agent. No one outside of law enforcement could explain the bitter acrimony that existed for the Stewards and no one inside of law enforcement would explain.

Orozco and Harrellson bristled, but Quad answered before either agent could put down the food they were holding or finish the bite they were chewing. "This is the Alpha of the Rare and Unknowns," he pointed at Ansel, "and that is his mate and by the smell of her she is of the line of Seraphine the War Elephant. Am I right?" he asked Imani, looking her dead in the eye.

Imani nodded once. Not bothering to hide her shock at being sniffed out by another shifter.

Quad whooped loudly but was quickly shushed by the movie watching crowd behind them. He grabbed Cinco around the neck and rubbed the teenager's head with his knuckles. "Son, did you bow before you sat down at the table? You're sitting with shifter royalty!" he exclaimed. "My wife is going to be so mad she went to wherever the hell she went instead of coming here tonight."

He let his son go turning back to Ansel and Imani. "I can't remember names or faces to save Cinco's life, but I can remember a shifter's scent twenty years after I meet them." His eyes sparkled.

Ansel had spent the last few moments staring off into space above Quad's head. He inhaled deeply. Imani could feel a soft swirl of magic from Ansel through the mating bond. They were definitely going to have a long conversation about each other's various abilities.

"You are one of mine." Ansel stopped, grabbing Imani's hand right as she was reaching for her monstrous sandwich creation. "One of ours, well both of you." Nodding his head at Cinco. "You're an Unknown. You came to my father twenty years ago to ask him to mediate a marriage contract dispute. I had to sit with him that day." Ansel paused trying to remember more of that day. "The father had said you could marry the daughter if you bested all her brothers in single combat." Stopping again, he rubbed the corner of his eye. "You did beat them all but were injured badly afterwards when they ganged up on you. It was a lot of brothers...like ten or fifteen. While you recovered which took months because they shattered your legs and hips. The father was trying to get out the contract because he had found a wealthier suitor. You were skinnier, much skinnier and were using canes, right?"

"Good job, Alpha. I'll excuse your earlier lapse as being distracted by your brand spanking new mate."

"That explains how you know his scent, but how do you know

mine?" Imani asked.

"Seraphine came here about twenty-five or thirty years ago to rain down pure Georgia hellfire on the Houston Herd for something. They Commune about five miles that way. We could feel her powers before we could see her; even from that far away." Pointing back toward the front of Pop's and the highway. "She stopped in here with the Houston Herd after their Commune. Her and Pop Trey instantly bonded. They spent the day playing cards, chess and dominoes until her flight back to Georgia that night. I was on butchering duty. They took turns yelling at me when it was time to pull things off the smoker." Quad smiled even wider. "Pop said no one had a better nose for smelling than an elephant, well after us." He tapped the side of his nose. "This thing isn't wide for nothing. I can smell everything from a lie to blood alcohol levels to cancer like a human bloodhound. Your grandmother could smell the moment that things were done and needed to come off the smoker." Quad was almost ecstatic.

Harrellson waived a hand after chanting for a few moments. The oak table and the benches lengthened making room for Jimmy and Zeke.

"That's kind of you, Agent. Too bad you couldn't teach me to do that to every table here. Be super useful on nights like tonight," Quad said thoughtfully.

Harrellson finished chewing a mouthful of macaroni and cheese. "It's no big deal. I was also tired of them staring at me." He started looking over his tray for more food. Finding none, he sighed disappointedly. "I'd give you a spell stone, but you know the use of magic for commercial use is strictly regulated. We'd have to get it patented and approved by the Office of Magical Patents and Objects which takes years. I'd be an old wizard and a retired Agent and one of your great-grandchildren would be in charge of the smoker by the time it was approved." Harrellson started wiping his fingers on a paper towel. "It's time to get you two back on the road to your destination."

"I don't think so," Ansel declared. He too, reached for the paper towels. He handed one to his mate and wiped his hands with the other he pulled from the roll.

"I do my best thinking when I'm airborne. While we were in the clouds, it hit me hard that this is not how two newly mated shifters should spend their first day together. Especially ones of our rank even if we aren't very concerned with rank right now. Newly mated shifters shouldn't be chaperoned by two Stewards, squashed into the trunk of their own car, taken far from their homes and families for an unspecified danger that you won't reveal to us. I've had enough with your inadequate protection."

Orozco stammered trying to find a rebuttal but failed. Harrellson begin turning a shade close to tomato red. Both Jimmy and Zeke howled with laughter, receiving a chorus of shushes in return.

Ansel continued, "Imani and I will be taking her car and checking into the hotel down the street after we hit the Target for essentials. I'm thinking that either you don't have enough magic between you two to stop us or Imani's magic repellent is too much for you to handle. If something or someone does come for us; I'll be Alpha enough to hide behind my mate because she can be scary, downright frightening as a human. I can't wait to see her War Elephant emerge; fully charged up and ready to take on the world."

Imani could feel the elephant dance a little jig at Ansel's words.

He unfolded his linebacker frame from the bench. He held a hand out to Imani as she stood alongside him. "Tomorrow, we will escort ourselves to the Stewards HQ in Houston. Good night all." With a gentle tug on Imani's hand, the couple begin to pick their way across the crowded clearing stepping over sleeping children, and blankets.

Chapter Nineteen

In An Our Now

At the car, Ansel opened the passenger door for her. "I cannot believe you just did that," Imani said. Wrapping her arms around his trim waist, she looked up at him. "You probably just broke about fourteen laws back there." She laid her head on his chest before asking, "Do mated shifters get sent to the same jail or are they separated?"

A low chuckle washed over her skin as he wrapped his arms around her in return. "I'll have our attorney file for a special dispensation. Mating frenzy does make a shifter kind of crazy, but I doubt we will be in trouble."

"Our attorney?" Imani said disbelievingly. "I'm in an 'Our' now."

"You definitely are in an 'Our' now, don't keep trying to get out of it either. I can feel your reluctance every now and then."

"I'll try to quash the reluctance, but only because I'm looking forward to a million orgasms."

Ansel threw his head back and howled with laughter. His deep voice carrying into the night enough that he received a chorus of "shhhhs" back from the movie watching crowd.

"Maybe, I should have promised the orgasms before my eternal love and devotion."

"I want those things too," Imani said getting into the car. Ansel leaned down buckling her seat belt.

"Princess, you already have them. You had them when you zapped me back shaking my hand that first day in the dining hall. My whole body felt like I'd been struck by one of my own bolts of lightning."

"You felt that too?"

He squatted down in the opening between the door and car. "Are you telling me you felt that spark and still walked away from me?"

"I felt it all over my body. Was it supposed to mean something?"

"That was the impundulu trying to claim you as our mate." He stood, closing the door. Walking around the back of the still deformed car, he got in on the driver's side. He just sat, face impassive not attempting to start the car or move.

Finally, he said, "I was sure that you had rejected us or that maybe you were already mated and that was why you walked away."

"I'm sorry, Ansel, it wasn't a rejection. I didn't know. Elephants don't do these things. We meet, ask each other a hundred questions. Decide together if we can tolerate the other person, then our Herds negotiate a marriage contract. Love, affection, attraction," she said ticking off each one on her fingers. "All that comes later for us, if it comes at all." She paused thinking of two of her aunt's loveless marriages.

"I've heard about other shifters having mating rituals and instant attractions, but I didn't pay attention to them. Because I was sure that one day I would be in a marriage because the bull passed the Herd's standards and the matchmaker thought we would be a good match."

"I only agreed to that farce Shifter Bachelor week my mother proposed because you had rejected me," he said quietly.

Chapter Twenty
Super Hero Training Begins

Ansel navigated her still magically deformed car into the sparsely filled parking lot of a Super Target. She realized that her purse and more importantly her wallet was in the missing portion of her trunk. "How much cash do you have? My wallet is in the missing part of the trunk." She regretted not putting her purse in the center console this morning.

She had asked Ansel softly. He was still feeling the rejection she had unwittingly given him two weeks ago in the dining hall. The mating bond pulsed with his disappointment. She had tried to hold his hand and send reassurance back through the bond. Ansel had shrugged her hand away in favor of resting it on the stick shift while he drove.

"Don't worry, I carry a few thousand dollars in cash with me everywhere."

"What? Why?"

"Not all of the Rare and Unknowns are as prosperous as Quad and his family with steady streams of income. Sometimes, I need to be able to buy a meal or diapers or pay a mechanic's bill."

"Will I need to carry that much cash? Will your people know me? Are you going to send out an email or something?"

Ansel chuckled. "Yeah, they will know you the same way they know me. Every shifter under my protection can either smell me out or find me like I'm magnetic north. My father, when he assumed the Alphaship, he had one of the more magically inclined shifters to create a spell for finding the Alpha as well as some other stuff. Through our bond, they'll feel you. No need for an email campaign."

"How do I help those who need help?" Imani asked. "I've never had to do stuff like this; elephant herds normally live within twenty miles of each other and we all know each other."

"The most important thing is to always listen; don't assume you know what they need. They are proud shifters, so even if you think you know what they want or need, you have to let them tell you what they want. I try to provide for immediate needs like groceries or a hot meal right then and there while I have them in front of me. I refer them to the staff in the offices for the long-term stuff like housing or a low interest car loan. If they are homeless, I delegate one of my security team to move them to one of the local offices. I'll introduce you to the staff when we get back to Marshall."

He got out of the car, coming around to the passenger side opening the door for her. Ansel helped her out, closed the door and grabbed her hand as they walked into the store. "The Alpha work is hard, I won't lie. Which is one of the reasons you have to have a great team. We have twenty-five offices around the world. Each is staffed by an Alpha in their own right, but they are Beta to me, well us."

"You have twenty-five Betas? That's unheard of! Do they each report to you on a daily basis?"

"They do. I thought I explained earlier to you, I only teach part time. I would love to be a full-time professor, but my alpha duties don't allow for it."

Before they walked inside, Imani asked. "Would you give up being Alpha if you could?"

Ansel exhaled, he pulled her into a hug, his hands naturally settling on her hips. Under her chin, she could feel his heartbeat speed up as their bodies drew close together. Her own heartbeat kicked into double time as she nestled her head into his neck. She breathed in his icehouse scent tinged with ozone while he answered. The smell of him and her brain projected images of her cuddled up on Ansel's lap. His ever-present erection stirred against her thighs. She marveled at his control. His mind was on speaking about a mundane subject, but his body was on action elsewhere. "I'm not sure. I've thought of it before. It's a difficult gig, but my father trained me for it from birth to assume the responsibility for our people and I can't think of anyone besides my sister, Cheryl who would even be up for the task. I'm like the governor of a small state that's spread all over the world. It might be easier if everyone lived in one area, but if wishes were fishes..."

She could feel her 'phant jerk her attention away from snuggling her nose deeper into Ansel's scent. The elephant sensed something watching. "Someone is watching us."

Ansel just chuckled. "I've been watching you all day, Princess. I like the sway of your hips when you walk. The way you blush, and it spreads halfway up your neck, but all the way down your chest. The way you attempt to distract me and the impundulu from this raging erection that is going to give me blue balls or something worse with Impundulu 101 questions." Imani felt a soft swirl of magic circling around them in a gentle breeze of velvet and smoke.

"No. This is serious. The 'phant feels ogled. You have to understand she is super sensitive to vibes in the air. War elephants evolved in the sixteen hundreds to stop human poachers from killing us wholesale and taking our ivory. Anyone who stares too long is a threat. If they don't stop, she might shift here and kill anything moving except maybe you. She kind of loves the hell out of you."

"When I asked you earlier how many War Elephants there had been, you said, 'In history or just right now?' now I want to know how many in history?"

"I'm a minute away from becoming a murderous killing machine and you want me to teach War Elephant History 101?"

Ansel smiled so broadly she could see that he still had his tonsils. "Well, I'll need to know it for our daughters," he teased. "Will my future baby girls turn into little armored warriors and wage battle in kindergarten class? That would be epic. They'll need a good foundation in military tactics before preschool."

"Alpha?" a timid voice asked from twenty feet away.

"Come closer, it's okay. I'm Ansel." He let go of Imani and gestured for the man to come closer. They met at the curb. "This is my new mate, Imani." Ansel held his hand out to the man.

They shook hands and the man smiled broadly. He was slightly built, maybe five feet three inches tall. He had shocking red hair, so bright and vibrant it was a technicolor marvel. Rivaling any sunset Imani had ever seen. His skin was so pale that it was almost translucent with deep green undertones. He looked like he was molting from the inside out and any day now the green would break through the skin and cover his whole body.

"I'm so pleased to meet you," he chirped, his voice had the burr of a Scottish accent. "I saw your father once when he was in my home country when I was a wee thing younger than most of my own children now." He pointed over his shoulder to a rusty green minivan where Imani could feel the stares of five little red haired almost green skinned children watching them back. "I don't remember him being so big though. Don't get me wrong he was huge, but you're like a giant."

Ansel just smiled and let the man continue talking.

"Alpha, my mate died giving birth to the wee babe six months ago and it's been rough since then. You know there just aren't a lot of shifter daycare centers, so I lost my job. With the green..." he held his hands out for them to see, "most humans won't hire me. I tell them it's a skin condition, hypochromic anemia like the manual tells us to, but they won't take a chance."

The 'phant dropped her murderous intentions; she couldn't help herself, she reached out touching the man; letting her healing powers wash over him. She could feel the infinite sadness in the man like a yawning chasm. There was no way for her to fill that space, but she wanted to provide a bridge, so he could walk over it.

He broke down in tears then. "I just want a job, so I can support my family. It's so hard with my mate gone to even get up in the morning, but I keep going because we have six little ones."

From somewhere out of his pocket, Ansel pulled a travel pack of tissues and handed it to him.

He fumbled with the pack and finally pulled one out. After wiping his tears, he continued, "We got evicted two days ago and spent the last two nights sleeping in the van. I just need some help, but I don't know what to do. Just as I was thinking of how much of a loser I am, a grown man who can't support his family. I felt you." He touched the space right above his heart. "I remembered that feeling from the time I saw your dad. It was like you were sent here to save me."

Out of another pocket, Ansel pulled out a pencil and small notepad. She made a mental note to check those shorts later for magicked pockets.

"Here, there is a BBQ place back that way," he pointed toward the general direction of Pop's. "Go there, ask for Quad. He's one of us. Tell him I sent you and to let you and the kids have whatever you want to eat. He can bill me at the main office. Then after everyone is full, there's a hotel." He pointed in the opposite direction. "Give me your name and number." Shoving the notepad and pencil into the man's left hand. "I'll reserve a room for you and the kids to stay. Tomorrow, I'll have someone, probably Cassie from the main office work on finding you somewhere to live, a job, and daycare."

He dutifully printed his name, Murphy MacBhaird and cell phone number in small neat letters then passed it back to Ansel.

"Alpha that's too generous. I can't accept all of that." The man gawked as Ansel was holding a wad of cash that had to have come from another magicked pocket.

"Murphy, you can, and you will, not for you, but for the littles." Nodding his head in the direction of the van. "You've paid your Alpha tribute? How many years have you paid your Alpha tribute?"

"Every year, my wife and I paid. It's what is expected of us."

Sticking the cash into Murphy's hands and wrapping his own hands around them. He said solemnly, "Don't think of this as charity. This is the return on your investment in me as Alpha. It is my job to protect you and I didn't do that very well for the last several months since your mate passed away. Let me fix that now."

Ansel pulled his hands away and left Murphy clutching the bills. "I can't guarantee that Cassie will be able to find you work in this area so you may need that for traveling money," Ansel said, with a cool passion like he had done this several hundred times. He reached into his magicked pockets again and pulled out several business cards.

"This," he held up a black card, "is my card with my personal cell." He gave Murphy two of them. "One for you and one for Quad since I forgot to give him one earlier." He held up a green card. "This is Cassie. She's the Talent Coordinator. Call her and talk to her. She'll find a job for you." He handed one last yellow card to Murphy. "This is Vernon. He will find you a home and a shifter sitter even if he has to come do it himself."

Murphy launched himself at Ansel, gathering him into the tightest hug Imani had ever seen. Ansel just hugged him back. Whispering words of encouragement and admiration that Murphy was still on his feet after losing a mate. There was a squealing sound of metal grinding on metal thirty feet from them. The sound irritated Imani's sensitive hearing until she spotted five flaming red heads of various heights bobbing across the parking lot toward them. They joined Murphy and covered Ansel in a wriggling mass of red and green group hug. He wrapped his long arms around them all and lifted the entire MacBhaird family off the ground to the delight of the children and even Murphy himself laughed out loud.

"Look Imani, it's the Power Rangers." He patted each one on the head. "Black Ranger, Blue Ranger, Green Ranger, Pink Ranger, Yellow Ranger. We are saved from the evil."

The youngest one barely came up to Ansel's knee. She giggled uncontrollably when he touched her head. "I'm not a Pink Power Ranger, Alphie."

Squatting down, he tossed her long fire curls over her shoulder from where she had been using them to hide her green hairline and cheeks. "You aren't the Pink Ranger? Who are you then?"

"I'm Colleen."

"Alright Colleen, if you want to keep your superhero identity a secret, I'll understand."

Colleen leaned closer, in a growly, stage whisper she replied, "It'll be our secret, Alphie, but I'm Batman."

She watched Ansel steel himself not to laugh at the pint-sized toddler, Colleen. His square jaw flexing and swallowing the laughter before it bubbled up and out. "Do you need a Robin?" he asked back seriously.

She shook her head side to side, her hair whipping around like a shampoo commercial.

Imani's hormones took another roller coaster ride. Her heart melted, while she could almost feel her ovaries start the ovulation process. She felt the mating bond thicken from the diameter of a jump rope to a soda can.

Ansel looked up at her, eyes sparkling. He stood to his full height, reaching for her hand. "Excuse us, Clan MacBhairds, but I need to take my mate shopping. Y'all have a great dinner, ok?"

He touched each child's head again, hugged Murphy with one arm and smoothly led her into the store. They left to a chorus of "byes" and the onset of Baby MacBhaird squalling from the mini-van.

"Well Alphie, I see you are ready to quit your day job to be Robin to a four-year-old girl's Batman. Highly irresponsible of you," she said with a straight face. Inside she was brimming over with laughter. Her hands automatically went to the shopping cart's handle, but Ansel quickly maneuvered it out of her way and pushed it toward the women's clothing section.

"Are you kidding? That would be the second best adventure of my life. Foiling candy thieves. Stopping toy rustlers. Late night snack cake heists."

Imani lost it, she could no longer contain her laughter. "My dad used to take me on midnight adventures to The Varsity and Waffle House and all kinds of all night places all over Georgia. He'd wake me up after Mom was asleep and we'd sneak out. No fighting toy rustlers though."

"Well, that's too bad. I'll make sure to take you on a midnight adventure for adult toys one night." Ansel said slyly. He waggled his eyebrows before he got momentarily distracted by a sequined sweatshirt on an end cap. His hands reached out to touch it before bringing them back to his sides as he steeled himself.

It was a moment before Imani understood, but he watched her face as she finally caught on to his double entendre. Her eyes widened just a bit while her body flushed halfway up the long column of her neck and all the way down her cleavage. The cool air of the store had her nipples standing at attention. His mouth watered just thinking of that blush creeping over her hardened nipples. He opened his mouth to say something even dirtier just, so she could blush deeper, but he felt her nervousness spike.

He stopped the red cart and moved it between two clothing racks, so it wouldn't continue down the aisle without them. He wrapped one arm around her waist. He felt his own nerves kick in and he had no idea why. The impundulu knew something and wasn't letting him in on the secret. For the millionth time, he wished the damn bird had regular emotions or was more effective communicating the ones he did have.

With his free hand, he titled her face up, so they could look each other directly in the eye. "I thought we were done with the reluctance on your part."

Imani paused a moment, then exhaled. Instead of pulling away as he thought she would do, she leaned in closer. She almost whispered, "Ansel, there is something I need to tell you. I've never played with toys in the adult way."

"No problem, Princess, I'll teach you all you need to know. We'll start small and then work our way up."

"Ansel, I'm a virgin."

Ansel felt as if someone had nailed his feet to the floor. "Never?" Ansel opened up all of his powers and senses and concentrated on his mate. He felt her do the same. He probed the edges of her power, overawed by the vastness of Imani's powers which dwarfed his. All Ansel felt was amusement coming from the impundulu. He had probably scanned her back at the Wolf Lodge while Ansel had been motivated with his heart and something two feet lower and to the right. The impundulu had used his mind. Ansel shaped his powers around Imani's body like he was making a plaster cast of her.

"I'm flattered that you waited so long for me."

"Don't be an ass. I wasn't trying to save myself for marriage. I tried to several times, but the elephant and I never agreed on the same guy at the same time."

Ansel felt his world tilt on the axis. He knew the next few moments were going to determine the rest of his life with Imani. "Do you want to wait until our wedding night?" he asked seriously wishing he didn't have too.

If she said yes, he knew it would be months before he could be alone with her. He could barely control himself now, half a day into their mating. The earliest they would be able to have a traditional wedding would be months from now. Months with no casual touching. Definitely, no making out like teenagers. No dates at his house. No dates at her place. They couldn't move in together. No sleeping beside one another even fully clothed. They would have to be chaperoned like toddlers. There would have to be a ten-foot buffer between them from this moment until some minister or judge legally pronounced them husband and wife. Eventually all the sexual tension that danced between them like a troupe of ballerinas would explode. He would have to take care of himself at least three times a day for months. He would need to buy coconut oil in vats.

All the while he would be desperate to see her. Smell her. Hear her laugh. Taste her. Bring her presents. Take her in the sky on his back. Feed her from his hand. Rub her skin.

It would be in a word.

Hell.

No Purgatory.

He looked down at her amber eyes shining up at him. The impundulu clearly said, 'We'll wait.' And he knew whether it was one month or one year, waiting for Imani would be worth any amount of time.

Chapter Twenty-One
Hibiscus & Grapefruit

They could feel her watching them. Neither he, nor the impundulu cared how silly she thought they were as they stood in the body wash aisle of Target. She leaned forward against the cart handle. Elbows resting on the metal bar, while her hands cradled her chin and her bright eyes sparked with mild amusement but more than a touch of boredom. Any minute she looked like she would lose her patience and cut a quick U turn taking off down the aisle to some other section. If he wasn't sniffing the seventeenth bottle of body wash trying to find the perfect scent to wash her; he would move her away from the handle. She kept trying to do things like that – lift heavy things, open the door herself.

He inhaled the scent of olive oil and verbena. Nope, not that one either. He grabbed the two he had set aside – hibiscus which had an undernote of cucumber and a honeyed grapefruit which would catch all the high notes of her natural scent.

"Two body washes?" she inquired. "Are both of those for me? I noticed you didn't get anything for yourself." Gesturing down the long aisle to the men's section.

"I use Ivory and only Ivory." He pointed into the cart where a four pack sat on top of the full cart of purchases.

"So, you can smell clean while I need to smell like I was dragged though the fruit section of the grocery store after being rolled around on the florist's floor at closing time?"

"Yes. Remember, I'm a bird brain and easily distracted by things like smell and reflective surfaces. You are my treasure and I want to be completely distracted by you."

He grabbed the basket and begin steering toward check out.

"You know I can push the cart by myself." She harrumphed.

"Yes, you are perfectly capable of it, but why would you need to when I'm here to do your bidding?"

The last two hours had been so educational for both of them. He knew her measurements down to her ring size and could be sent anywhere on the planet and buy her a whole new wardrobe now. He knew what size dress and what styles she preferred. For all the good it did, she could care less about dressing up or even her casual clothes. Athletic gear, on the other hand was a whole different kettle of fish. She'd spent at least twenty minutes feeling for microscopic differences in the moisture wicking abilities of two shirts. Then another twenty feeling for the same differences in yoga pants. Ansel had eventually snatched them all from her and tossed them into the shopping cart.

To his absolute horror, she preferred comfortable shoes over sexy ones. They briefly argued in the shoe section before 'compromising' as he tossed all three pair into the cart – two tennis shoes and one pair of heels. He had been right earlier, when he had been speculating that she wore no bra under her tank top. Her favorite color was a seafoam green, and that she really, truly detested not being the person pushing the shopping cart. That she thought he was a thief for eating grapes as they shopped. She liked beef jerky and cheese as a snack while he liked fruit and nuts.

As they approached the front of the store, Ansel steered straight for the open cashier and begin tossing items from the shopping cart onto the belt.

Chapter Twenty-Two
A Shifter With A Mission

Imani just gave up and followed Ansel's lead. He was a shifter with a mission and she only had one choice. Follow willingly or get dragged behind him. After they checked out at Target, he'd grabbed all twenty-seven bags in his left hand and her hand with his right and begin speed walking out of the store. The passenger door was opened and before she could blink, she found herself buckled in with the bags tossed in the "backseat".

They zoomed out of the parking lot on two wheels. Less than ten minutes later they pulled up to the hotel. Once again, Ansel grabbed all the bags with one hand and was pulling her into the lobby. She paid little attention to Ansel checking them in. She spent her time admiring the long leanness of Ansel as he leaned into the high counter as he booked a suite for the MacBhairds.

His broad shoulders and back tapered into a wide 'v'. His cargo shorts hung low on his lean hips covering his tight ass and muscular thighs. From the top of his head to his boat shoes shod feet Ansel was all smooth, creamy midnight black skin that she wanted to drag her fingertips across then her tongue to see if that licorice was edible. She fisted both of her hands, so she wouldn't be tempted to run her hands over his skin. Desire flared through her knocking out any residual nervousness. She had feared this day for so long thinking she would finally lose her virginity to a virtual stranger. Some random bull elephant the Herd had picked for his Herd's connections rather than his heart. Not once in all her imagining about the future had she believed that there was a destined soulmate for her. Specifically, a future mate like Ansel who although very much an Alpha's Alpha was kind and generous to his core. She had never hoped to have a love match like her parents and especially an all enduring love match like her grandparents whose love and devotion had stopped a war in its tracks. Love like her parents and grandparents were special once in a lifetime romances that weren't promised to everyone.

"Are you ready?" he whispered into her ear.

She looked up to see Ansel standing next to her. He smiled all white teeth and gleaming midnight skin. Her insides dropped.

"I'm ready."

Upstairs in the hotel room, they both undressed in seconds. Ansel grabbing the bag with body washes and soap. Together, they walked hand in hand into the bathroom. Ansel turned on the shower, while Imani opened the Ivory soap and carefully curated bottles of body wash discovering sea sponges she hadn't even noticed nestled inside the bag.

Ansel turned from getting the water piping hot. The steam rising up the glass column of the shower and to the ceiling. "Imani, I've been playing it cool as I could all day but with both of us here and naked. I'm not sure how long I'll be able to last. You've been the star of every dream I've had the last couple of weeks. I might explode if you touch me too much. Let me wash myself then you. I'm not sure I could handle your hands all over me right now." His eyes roamed her body with a naked lust that sent sparks of elation shooting through the elephant.

"O kay." She gestured to the floor. "Should I wait right here or go back into the room?"

"Wait right here. Don't move a muscle." Ansel stepped backwards into the shower. She watched his hands as he vigorously rubbing the bar of Ivory onto the sea sponge. He started washing his neck then continued down his chest all the way to his navel. Imani stood enthralled watching the bright yellow sea sponge against his rich, dark skin.

She had seen naked men her entire life. Most shifters disrobed en masse in their familial groups. However, Imani had never reacted to a man's body the way she reacted to Ansel. Everything about him and his body drove her and the elephant's instinct to couple and mate. Who was she kidding? He could have here on the floor of the bathroom. She wanted to lay on the floor right here waiting for him to finish washing. He could step out and lay right on top of her. Or she could climb Ansel like a ladder. The plunge herself down onto his massive erection until she was irrevocably deflowered.

Ansel turned his body; yellow sponge being dragged down the length of his leg. Imani turned to gather her own shower supplies enthusiastically waiting for the moment that she could step under the shower's spray.

He took one final turn under the water then stepped out taking everything from her and tossing all into the tub. Roughly, he gathered her in his arms. Lifting her higher into his arms, her legs wrapped around his waist as he carried her into the shower. His mouth pressed to hers gently, lips firm he kissed her long and deep. She felt the cool tiles along her back and the intense heat of Ansel along her front. Again, she took the lead shoving her tongue into his mouth. Her hands sliding to every part of his exposed skin she could caress.

Time had no meaning for them as they stood under the scalding hot water. They kissed like they were sharing the same bubble of oxygen, greedily. Her hands explored everywhere she could reach his pecs, his back, the upper curve of his tight ass. Twice she had opened her eyes to see if Ansel had grown more hands because she felt caressed everywhere at the same time, but Ansel's hands were slow moving instruments of pleasure. He didn't rub her skin, her caressed and kneaded her muscles. One long sexually charged deep tissue massage.

Only when the water was lukewarm did they stop kissing and fondling one another. Ansel grabbed another sponge lathering furiously. He grabbed both of her wrists in one massive hand and raised them over her head. Then he started to gently wash her. He hummed softly to himself as he skimmed the sponge over every inch of her skin.

He kissed her deeply as the soap rinsed from her body. Her knees were pudding and she could barely hold herself upright. Ansel again lifted her, carrying her out of the shower straight to the bed.

"One stroke, a moment of pain and then a million orgasms to come," he whispered softly as he lay her down and climbed over. He reached for her painfully swollen clitoris, it quivered under his slight touch. She moaned as one of his fingers opened her entrance. Her sexual experience was very limited, but she knew the pleasure one finger could bring. Ansel didn't stop at one finger, a second then third finger joined in. Opening her further than she had ever been opened before.

"You aren't ready for me yet, Princess. I can fix that." He backed off the bed. His fingers opening her lips for his mouth to descend. All the air in her lungs left her body with the first flick of his tongue. Davida had explained and explained the pleasure, but she had never imagined a man's mouth on her would make her want to float off the bed into a cloud of vapor. He kissed her down there the way he kissed her mouth, lots of tongue, gentle nips and something new, a gentle sucking vacuum that was her new favorite thing in the universe. An orgasm shuddered through her and Ansel doubled the speed of his tongue. She grabbed his head, her nails gauging crescent moon shapes into his scalp as she crested the wave of one orgasm and spiraled directly into a second more powerful one.

She felt his low chuckle against her vulva moments before he sucked her painfully swollen clit into his mouth. At the same time, he stood up bringing her hips with him. Her entire being was locked into one position, Ansel's. She was dangling down the front of his body boneless. Only her shoulders touched the bed and he never let go of her hips, but somehow pushed her legs down and over his shoulders. His mouth became a Dyson vacuum cleaner. She screamed as she felt her body convulse again. Ansel laid her back on the bed. She looked up at him through her lashes. He was smiling his all teeth megawatt smile at her.

"I think you're ready for me now, Cookie." He walked over to the table and grabbed two bottles of water.

"Tomorrow, I'll shave you. There should be no hair between your legs except my beard."

Her mouth was open, but no words came out. The impundulu's

amusement could be felt through the mating bond and Ansel's was evidenced by his ear to ear grin. He chugged his bottle of water. Imani ignored the offered water.

"Drink up, Princess, I'm just getting started."

This time he crawled up her body from the foot of the bed and nestled his hips into the junction of her thighs.

"This is my last offer to be a gentleman. If you want to wait until our wedding night, then you need to say something in this moment."

She pulled his face down to her and kissed him as passionately as she could. He positioned himself at her entrance. A moment of trepidation passed through her, should they wait? The elephant took the decision from her by raising her hips and impaling them onto Ansel.

Chapter Twenty-Three
A Million To Go

Imani lay panting. Her magnificent chest rose and fell mirroring his own breathing. "There is one other thing we need to do," he said slowly not sure how she would react to the last step.

"It's okay, where do you have to bite me?"

"Bite you?"

"Yeah for your mark."

"I'm a lightning bird not a werewolf." He scoffed.

"You want to strike me with lightning?" Imani begin trying to sit up. Panic rising in her chest. "That will be a no. People die getting struck by lightning."

He raised his hand next to his face and let the electricity pulse between his fingers like a nebula ball. "I, well we need to run a current from me into you building up until we reach the full power of one of my lightning bolts running between us."

"It's going to run through you into me?"

"Did you think I was just going to strike you with a bolt of lightning?" Ansel demanded.

"Well yeah," Imani replied sheepishly.

He felt her body relax beneath him. "I would never harm you, Princess." He grabbed her hands, interlacing their fingers. Taking extra care to make sure their palms were in full contact with each other, he pushed a small current from his right hand into her left. She gasped as the current begin to flow slowly through her body.

He could see her curly hair rising off the pillow. He increased the current and smiled when he heard her deep moans begin again. Her pussy grasped him tighter and tighter. Leaning in, he turned the volume of the electrical current up to match the rhythm of his strokes into Imani's silkiness. Faster and faster he pushed the flow of electricity into her left palm and drew it back out of her right palm. The faster he needed to push himself into Imani.

Why did he believe that this would be like normal sex? Ansel fought the urge to let go of their joined hands, so he could grab her thighs, pushing her knees up to her ears so he could feel her spasming around his shaft while he drove himself deeper and deeper into her.

The impundulu thought one word "Slow." He could feel the impundulu underneath his skin. His eyes were the obsidian black of his inner animal.

Taking deep breathes, he slowed the rhythm of his strokes into Imani's heat. Every fifth stroke he increased the electrical surge. He clutched her hands tighter as he felt her orgasm commence. He threw his head back and rode the waves of her seventh and largest orgasm of the night. Her whole body shook like a tremor. She gasped for air while whispering his name over and over. One final stroke and one final push of lightning and Ansel emptied himself into Imani. Everything he had and everything he would have was hers to keep.

Chapter Twenty-Four

Dream Mate

Imani's soft and curvaceous body fit into all the hard places of his body like a well-made puzzle locking together. Turning his head slightly he admired the riot of chocolate and blonde curls that seemed to explode from her scalp as she rested her head on his shoulder. Now he understood why she kept it pulled back in that same too tight bun.

He decided that this was the best moment of his entire life. For the last two decades, he had imagined what his future mate would be like. He was even pickier than his twin sister, Cheryl who had a dream mate list that was longer than her left leg. Anything physically or emotionally or even personality wise he had ever liked or admired in another woman was all here is spades in Imani.

Bright eyes. Imani's eyes were so bright they looked like they had to have a separate power source.

Sarcasm. She had to have a degree in it, and she used it like a weapon.

Thick thighs and long smooth legs.

Offbeat sense of humor. She was her own comedy special.

Show stopping smile. The first time and every time since she had smiled at him It had felt like a sunrise. His own personal sunrise.

Curvy body. His eyes and hands would never get their fill of just looking at her.

Intelligence.

Fiercely independent.

Deep dimples. You could swim laps in them.

Patience, well mostly.

Hopefully, she also had never ending capacity for love.

She sighed deeply and snuggled closer to his chest and threw one of her legs over his legs. He might melt from the joy it gave him having her so close and so comfortable that she was treating his body like her own personal chaise lounge.

There was only one thing he wanted. It was too early, but he felt like he'd waited twenty years and couldn't do another day. Even another hour was too long. "Imani, tell me you love me."

She went from utterly relaxed almost boneless in his arms to stiff as a board in a heartbeat. Instantly, he regretted asking.

He could feel the gears of her brain kicking into gear as she sat up. She grabbed the sheet to cover herself. He saw one last glimpse of her half dollar sized nipples before she tucked the sheets into her armpits.

"Ansel, are we supposed to fall deeply madly truly in love during sex? Or during the mating frenzy?" she stalled.

"No. It happens though but I had hope that you would be willing to say the words."

"I can't lie. I'm very attracted to you. I like you as a person, but elephants take our time with love."

"I've waited for you for twenty years, Imani. Just say the words." His impatience and that of the impundulu was running out. This woman had rejected him several times already that first day in the dining hall.

"No, you've waited on the idea of me. Twenty years ago, I was eight-years-old. A third grader doesn't make a good mate. You realize we only just mated this morning. If it's been twelve hours, I'd be completely floored."

"What do elephants do to fall in love?"

"The Centumrogatio."

He frowned hard. Actually, felt his face fold up into hard lines. "I failed Latin in high school and what I remember isn't very good."

She dimpled back smiling. "When interviewing prospective mates, we each ask fifty questions — the rogatio. Together they make up a centum."

"I just write any fifty questions?"

"No. The questions are already written; this is at least a five centuries old tradition for elephants. They'll come up randomly on the app."

"There's an app?" He needed to get used to shifters who adopted human technology. His shifters were very old school, so much difference between her Herd and the R & U. "How?"

"My cousin created it. I sat in on the grant meeting. He figured with the elephant population exploding world-wide over the last decade we would need a way to do it without carrying the book around or waiting to get to the book, it costs four dollars and ninety-nine cents. I don't know any single elephant shifter, who doesn't have it. I think he made the money back on the grant with the first one hundred downloads."

They did business grants? He wanted to pick her brain about how the elephants got rich and stayed rich. He could and would use all of the ideas for the Rare and the Unknows. It would have to wait until later. Much later. He needed to convince her that he loved her, and she could love and would love him, and they were a perfect fit for each other.

She rose from the bed. Pulling the sheet with her and trailing behind her. The sheet covered nothing except her armpits and the tops of her breasts. Her gorgeous back, plump ass and shapely legs was available for his purview. He stretched back across the bed and watched her turn on her phone after unplugging it from the charger and begin flipping through screens. She stood with one foot on the floor her other leg leaned against her knee.

"Found it." Turning around, the sheet tangling around her ankles and legs like a Greek statute. She paused for a couple of breaths, then begin reading. "Ansel Adams Junaid will you complete the Loxodonta tradition of the Centumrogatio with me?" She kept reading not pausing to wait for his answer. "You must know that once we have begun, we cannot stop until the last question has been asked and answered. The Centumrogatio can take between three hours and eight hours or, even longer. There can be no outside interruptions of the Centumrogatio, and we must look into each other's eyes as we both ask and answer each question. Each question must be answered truthfully. One lie can ruin the ritual. If after we have completed all the discussion questions and we agree that there is no chance for life, love and true happiness between us we will part as friends."

"Yes, Imani Seraphine Wilson, I will complete the Loxodonta tradition of the Centumrogatio with you. I hope by the end your feelings will mirror mine," he answered as formally as she had asked. He had felt the tradition of the words and phrasing even though he was sure the statement had been updated for the modern app.

She looked indecisive. "Bed? Sofa?"

"How about you get dressed? I'll order some room service then we can begin after the food gets here. No interruptions." She looked relieved, but he felt her stress levels rise again.

"Have you ever done the Centumrogatio?"

"I almost asked someone once when I was seventeen. I had the book, markers and the dice in my backpack. We were supposed to meet after school, but I couldn't find him. I went looking and found him kissing Karen Kirkendahl. First, she's a dragon shifter and elephants and dragons are mortal enemies. Second, she's a skank of the first degree. Third, I wanted no part of him after that."

He couldn't help but laugh and thank fate for putting Karen Kirkendahl in the path of that poor dude.

Forty minutes later they sat at the small table covered with seventeen plates of food and snacks. No alcohol was allowed during the ritual.

"Let's do this." He rubbed his hands together. "Who goes first?"

"Normally in elephant tradition the woman goes first, but for the Centumrogatio the man goes first." She offered him her phone.

"Go bring your charger closer. Don't want it to die halfway through the ritual." She ran to get the charger.

"There's a spinner. Hold your finger down on it as long as you want, and it will choose a question," Imani instructed as she came back to the table.

Ansel held his finger down for three seconds. The first question appeared. He read over it and felt his stomach drop. These were not the 'What's your favorite color?' or 'Book that changed your life?' questions. These were the bare your soul and see if you are worthy questions.

"If you knew that in one year you would die suddenly, would you change anything about the way you are now living? Why?"

"If you asked me that a year ago, I would have said that I wouldn't want to die a virgin." She blushed as she said it. "Now I would say that I wouldn't want to die estranged from my mother and Herd as a Rogue. Elephants don't do well alone. It's almost a codependence that we have a compulsive need to be around or at least near each other."

"You'll never be alone, as long as I'm alive. I'll be worse than a toddler underfoot." He watched her eyes sparkle as she giggled.

He passed the phone back to her. She swiped the question to the left. He saw the colorful spinner flash. She tapped the spinner for two seconds. He discretely hoped for an easy question.

"What's the worst thing you have ever down to another person and why? Do you regret it?"

"Before I answer, tell me are there any easy questions? Are they all like this?"

She didn't even bother to answer. Just shook her head side to side.

Lifting his eyes to meet her amber orbs. He braced himself to watch the light die in them. "I killed the man who murdered my father after he lost in fair combat during the Alpha challenge. I also banished his entire family from the Rare and the Unknown. I regret nothing."

Chapter Twenty-Five
Orgasm is a Breakfast Food

Imani awoke clinging to Ansel's broad shoulders like a monkey. Her arms wrapped around his chest and one leg over his hip. Quickly, she disentangled herself from his still slumbering body. She stood to stretch. Her body; she was deliciously sore everywhere from Ansel's ministrations. As quiet as she could, she gathered a few items from the still unpacked Target bags before she headed to the bathroom to shower.

Just as her skin was fully damp from the showerhead, moments before she was about to soap her body, the shower curtain pulled back to reveal a sleepy-eyed, but smiling Ansel.

"Good morning, Mate, new day, new orgasm," he announced as he stepped into the shower with her and snatched her loofah out of her hand. He tossed it over his shoulder. "I've got something better to wash you with." Holding his hands in front of her. "Give me the soap."

Without a word, she dropped the bar of soap into his hands and turned, giving him her back. He lathered his hands before gently starting with her neck, kneading the muscles with his fingertips. At her first moan, he moved to her shoulders then lower to her waist, then her backside. He gathered the soap again, running his large hands over it several times. Kneeling, he massaged the backs of her thighs and calves.

"While, I'm here I might as well have breakfast," he murmured before plunging his face between her parted thighs. His tongue swirled her folds.

Her knees buckled, but Ansel was there to catch her. He pulled her hips out further as his tongue explored more of her folds before caressing her clitoris. He alternated suckling her then laving his wide tongue over her. Through the mating bond, he felt her body's response before it responded. The impundulu screamed inside of him in triumph as Imani's orgasm descended. His tongue greedily lapped at her opening.

Standing, Ansel helped her turn until she was facing him. He kissed her parted lips before lifting her up and sliding his hands under her bottom. With one, swift stroke he entered her before her first orgasm was complete. Short quick strokes and she was melting in his arms again. He kept going until he felt his own orgasm cresting. His seed flowed out of him like lava deep into Imani.

Chapter Twenty-Six
Beware The Tusks

Imani steered her car into the parking lot of the headquarters of the Shifters & Magic Task Wardens— or as they are more commonly referred to Stewards. The square red brick building loomed out of the flat Texas landscape buttressed on three sides by a quirky turn in the Trinity River. Unlike the FBI Headquarters in Washington, DC you couldn't even tell if this was the actual headquarters of a national law enforcement agency until you read the discreet sign over the regular looking set of glass doors.

Imani had seen grocery stores with more security measures. There was no security implements visible anywhere on the outside, video cameras, motion sensors or security barriers and metal detectors. Even the inside of building looked more suited to polite tax accountants and anxious probate attorneys, with its worn, beige and burgundy paisley printed carpets, tasteful abstract paintings in glossy black frames and one lone security guard sitting behind a low table. The white shirted guard looked so bored and sleepy if you weren't looking you would have thought he was asleep. He leaned back on two legs in his chair casually flipping through a magazine. He didn't even look up or react when Ansel held one of the glass doors open for Imani as they walked in.

As they were halfway across the small lobby, just as Ansel was about to introduce them to the guard and ask for Special Agents Orozco and Harrellson's supervisor. A dozen different alarms started screaming on different auditory frequencies. One of the alarms was set so high, he could feel the impundulu screaming, tearing at his ears. The pain so intense, it caused Ansel to fall to his knees. Grabbing his ears, Ansel too screamed in pain. The guard casually looked up at Imani to discover her still on her feet unperturbed by the alarms.

The magazine fell from fingers rapidly transforming into the paws of a massive polar bear who smashed the desk to charge directly at Imani. The War Elephant inside of Imani laughed maniacally. She needed a fight and this freaking polar bear looked like he would make a lovely rug for her and her mate to snuggle on in front of the fire.

She blurred the line between human body and her true form before the girl could grasp the magic rising. As she shifted, she felt ceiling debris rain down on her sides as she rose to her full height of twenty-five feet tall. She saw the change in the bear's eyes as it went from fury to fear. The fully charging bear tried to stop its charge, but like a cartoon character on ice; its momentum was too fast across the marble floor and it went ass over tea kettle directly into the War Elephant who stood unfazed as thirteen hundred pounds of bear hit her in the ankles. The bear was unconscious from the impact and lay sprawled at her feet. She turned to see her mate still on the floor cowering under the high-pitched frequencies of the alarms. She pushed her magical immunity through the mating bond. Moments later, Ansel stood as his healing powers corrected the damage to his eardrums.

He walked over, laying hands on the hard marble like texture of her hide. "You're even more amazing than I imagined from the description you gave me back at the Wolf Lodge." He ran his hands lightly over her as he walked toward her head.

"Don't touch the tusks, we were serious when we said they were like ivory scimitars."

Ansel stood flummoxed with one hand caressing an ear that looked like a marble statue. Staring directly into that burnt amber eye, he forgot all about her dangerous tusks and the smooth texture of her hide. "You can talk. You speak in animal form!" he screamed in a high-pitched excited voice; that wasn't anywhere near his normal baritone speaking voice.

"I told you elephants do things differently and that the War Elephants do whatever they want. How can I command battle forces in battle with no voice?"

The wall behind where the security guard sat suddenly slid to the side revealing a fully armed squadron of a dozen shifter special forces dressed in navy blue tactical gear aiming anti-tank missiles at them.

Imani warned Ansel, "Stand behind me!"

Ansel scrambled behind Imani as he heard the high-pitched whine of the rockets being fired at them. He felt the room quiver, but the noises didn't deafen him. Whatever the War Elephant had done through the mating bond, his hearing was no longer sensitive to the loud noises or certain frequencies that had driven both him and the impundulu insane with pain before.

The War Elephant taunted them as the smoke cleared. "Is that all you have? I could have taken that in human form. You brought only guns to fight me. Where are your warriors with teeth and claws?" She laughed manically again, this time the sound was out loud for everyone to hear.

The sound of that insane laughter shredded Ansel's nerves to microscopic bits. That laugh sent icy shivers of death stalking down his spine. It made all the hair on Ansel's body stand on end before he rippled as his actual downy under feathers sprouted on his arms and legs in fear and alarm. Even the impundulu froze, petrified by the sound of her laughter.

Every instinct both human and animal said flee. There was no fight here he could win; only a losing fight for his short and very brief survival. His body tensed to run, to change and fly. To run as far and as fast as his body could carry him. He needed to take to the sky; flying as far as his wings could take him.

The laugh had to be a war tactic because it scared him senseless. He wanted to run and never look back, but he knew Imani and the War Elephant weren't insane, but that laugh sounded like the best and worse villain laughs in all the movies he'd ever watched.

Apparently, he surmised, the fully armed squadron didn't know his mate as well as he because they collectively dropped their weapons and ran in the opposite direction deeper into the building.

"I hope you've had your fun now, Imani," a clear but heavily accented voice asked through the speaker system.

"Not really. Is that really all of the resistance they're going to put up?" the War Elephant said casually as if she was waiting for a cup of coffee in a café.

"I tried to warn them that there were some shifters who couldn't be brought down by anti-tank weapons, but who wants to listen to the little old woman seer."

"Oh, The Seer," the War Elephant said it like a snake stretching those four syllables easily into sixteen. "My grandmother has told me stories about you. Are you all the legends say you are?"

"Is your grandmother all the legends say she is?" the Seer snapped back. "Do you think you are really improving the War Elephant legacy by getting shot with a dozen anti-tank missiles and ripping through twenty-five magical wards some over a hundred years old?" she chastised Imani. "Now change back and bring your mate upstairs to meet me. There's an elevator to the right of you. Fifth floor."

The War Elephant expelled a burst of frustrated air out of her spiked trunk. She looked around for something to pulverize. The closest thing was the unconscious form of the still shifted polar bear guard. Although, she really wanted to fight – there was no one to fight and she wasn't going to fight someone who couldn't fight back.

She stomped one giant foot, shattering the concrete from her giant foot outwards of thirty feet away. Concrete stalagmites poked upwards through the carpet like shark teeth. The entire lobby had been thoroughly destroyed within what seemed like a minute, but Ansel knew it had been more like ten minutes. Exposed ceiling tiles and wires hung down like balloon streamers. The sheetrock appeared to be splashed with acid the way shrapnel from the anti-tank missile had peppered the walls after they detonated against Imani's hide then splatted. Larger pieces of shrapnel had shot everywhere like an angry porcupine had shot all its quills at once. With one last flourish, she raised her trunk and trumpeted her battle call. It shook the building causing more debris from the ceiling to fall on them.

Just as quickly as she had appeared, the War Elephant disappeared, leaving a heavily breathing Imani in her place. Other than her breathing, Imani had been unaffected by the damage around them. Even the dust from the ceiling didn't fall on her. Ansel offered her a hand to lift her out of the two-foot depression her stomp had left in the floor. A dozen questions stampeded to the front of his mind, but the one that tumbled out first was. "How are you still dressed?"

"I thought I explained the War Elephant does what she wants, and she doesn't want to be naked. Dignity is the first trait we elephants learn."

"Are you really insane or is that laugh just to scare people?" Ansel asked next. He looked down at his arms and legs still clad in two layers of his soft, downy under feathers. "I haven't fledged out like this in fear since I was a fledging maybe three or four years old. I'll confess that laugh stopped my heart and made my mind turn off. All rational thought just left me, I didn't know whether to run or run."

"I'll never tell."

"Oh Princess, that's crazy sexy right there." He allowed his eyes to roam over the lines of the red dress she had allowed him to pick for her. The V-neck dress was cut just low enough that he could see the cups of the lacy bra they had finally found at Target last night. His body, even though still frightened to his core, reacted again to hers. He could feel his length harden at the thought of her using that laugh.

I'm a goner, he thought again. *Complete and total goner.*

Imani snorted. The mating bond pulsed with his desires and she shivered. He did too with delicious thoughts of his broad, thick length driving into her soreness. His strong hands with his long tapered fingers gripping her thighs. "I think, I should be the one doing the asking, 'who's the sane one?' in this relationship."

She headed for the now magically revealed elevator doors. Ansel following behind, arms still covered in onyx downy feathers.

Once inside, he hit the button for the fifth floor. Imani asked, "Is this what your warrior form looks like?"

"I don't have a warrior form," he admitted.

He would tell her later over a couple of bottles of wine while feeding her tidbits of fruit and cheeses about trying to force the impundulu into a warrior form when he was thirteen. After, she was tipsy, he would explain how all he managed to do was get stuck with feathers in all the most uncomfortable places for a week and an angry impundulu seething at him.

"Then how do you battle?" she asked, head slightly tilted.

"In animal form as the impundulu, he wouldn't have it any other way." He debated grabbing her again to suck on her full, pouty bottom lip, but she had taken her time this morning carefully applying her makeup like a professional. If they weren't about to meet an actual living legend, he would say to hell with it. He definitely would mess her whole face up, lipstick smeared. Eye shadow smudged. Hair standing both on end and falling out of her chignon. She would leave this elevator with her dress off her shoulders, hem up to her waist and her panties in his pocket.

"Really." She lounged against the back wall of the elevator completely relaxed. Her hip on the brass railing, legs straight only for the purpose of holding her up. Not bracing like most people riding an unfamiliar elevator. He checked the mating bond, her self-assurance knew no bounds when the War Elephant was close to the surface. He felt the elephant prowling the mating bond with the impundulu chasing her. How their animals found new ways to play with each other through the magic completely floored him.

He sighed reluctantly.

She glanced over at him and boldly said, "You're a sex crazed fifteen-year-old boy, aren't you?"

"Am not. I'm a sex crazed shifter who is in the midst of a mating frenzy and still being denied exploring his mate's body and marking her orgasms on my mental tally. A fifteen-year-old would only be focused on his completion. I'm focused on your orgasms."

She blushed. Eyes downcast, she murmured, "How long does the mating frenzy last?"

"It depends on the species, I've heard stories of three days to six months."

"Six months like last night?" she breathed. Her insides melted under the lecherous look that spread across Ansel's face.

He just nodded.

She could feel her body heating again.

The elevator doors slid open revealing a diminutive white-haired lady swathed head to toe in red. Red sweater, red pants and red shoes with a red and black tartan scarf thrown casually around her neck. The strong, clear voice from the lobby speaker welcomed them. "I'm glad you both were able to make it. Nothing harder than trying to get the full attention of newly mated shifters. I know I've tried, it's all bedroom, bedroom, bedroom with them."

She turned right, proceeding them down a stark white hallway. "Follow me. I had them disable most of the magic on this section of the floor. Hopefully, it's done correctly. When Sera gets here, it'll be such a test of the magic of the building..."

"My grandmother is coming, here?" Imani stopped walking, foot paused in the air.

"Your grandmother is on her way, with your mother, grandfather and any Herd member who can hold warrior form."

Ansel laughed at Imani's expression. "Family to the rescue!"

Imani shot him a side eye that would seer flesh off bone. The smile dropped off his face.

The Seer said to Ansel, "Your mother, sister and entire security team are riding with the Herd. I believe they chartered a private jet or a cargo plane."

It was Imani's turn to laugh. "Security team to the rescue!" She had learned during the Centumrogatio that the thing Ansel hated most about being Alpha was his security team. He and Stanley, the Head of Security were best friends since they were in diapers only made it bearable. Just having to have the team still bristled Ansel's feathers, he felt he could protect himself, but his people had voted and upped their own yearly fees to cover the cost.

Ansel groaned at the news. "Why are my mother and sister coming?"

"I called them. The danger hasn't passed because you've found a mate," she said as she led them into a small conference room with a round black table with four chairs, dark grey carpet and more, unadorned white walls.

Ansel pulled a chair out for the ladies before he lowered himself into the uncomfortable chair. The tops of his thighs scrapped the underside of the low table. Imani had the same problem so they both pushed back from underneath the table. "What is this danger and why is it so big that you are trying to keep me from properly mating?" He gestured above his head. "I've had it up to here with the whole, 'Danger! Danger! Danger!' I just want to take my mate and disappear for a month."

"The danger isn't a what anymore. It's a who. Her name is Mahjabeen. She is one of the oldest practitioners of dark magic in the world. She wants you and through your Alpha bond to the one point seven million shifters of the Rare and Unknowns to turn all of you into her personal army."

"No magic worker in the world is strong enough to do that on their own." He stood. "Come on, Imani. This was a waste of time."

"Alone she isn't, but she has a super coven."

"That's illegal. I shouldn't have to tell the Stewards how to do their jobs, but you..."

"Sit down, Ansel," the Seer commanded.

Boneless, Ansel dropped into the chair.

"I exerted very little magic in that command. Not because I wanted to prove a point, but just because I have very little magic. Anyone strongly versed in magic manipulation will be able to take advantage of you while you are in you mating frenzy."

Imani ignored the cold glares that Ansel was giving the Seer and the flint like glares, the Seer was giving him right back across the cheap conference room table. "How does she have a super coven?

They are illegal. It's illegal for that many magic users to gather, correct?"

"She found a loophole. It took her forty years to exploit it, but she has a super coven and there is nothing we can do to shut it down."

"WHY NOT? Do you know the danger to my kind? There are only two dozen of us," Ansel exploded. He stood, hands balled into fists grinding into the particle board covered table, leaving divots everywhere he touched.

Imani touched his arm, while whispering for him to calm down.

"I will not calm down. They're out there waiting to take me and slaughter my kind and enslave our people."

"Ansel be quiet!" the Seer commanded. "Let me finish explaining." She took two deep breaths calming herself. "When we passed the laws against super covens, we – well they didn't take into account one witch or warlock having enough magical children to form a super coven. Just like in shifters, the magic doesn't pass automatically to every child. We can't stop the super coven from assembling because, you can't stop family reunions. She had twenty-seven children. Lucky for her and unlucky for the rest of the world, only fourteen of them are powerful enough magicians to stand in the coven."

Ansel plopped into the chair and leaned forward onto the round table with his elbows. Eyes round with the implications of the Seer's words. His downy feathers which had started to recede back into his skin, puffed out again.

"Three is the magic multiplier. All of their magic combined will be exponentially greater by a factor of fifteen. They can take me and through me have an army of almost two million shifters to do whatever they want through the Alpha bond."

Through the mating bond, Imani felt his fear for all of his people being forced into the same magical servitude as his great grandparents.

"What can we do?" Imani asked. "We can't stay hidden here and we can't remain hidden forever. Why can't my magical immunity protect Ansel?"

"I had speculated incorrectly it seems, that once you two were mated – some if not all of your magical immunity would be conveyed to Ansel. The things I witnessed Sera do to Joseph when he was injured during the Great War had me convinced that your immunity would protect Ansel and by extension all of the Rare and Unknowns."

"My grandparents had been married over twenty years, no closer to thirty years during the great war. Besides, my grandfather is a wereelephant. How could you just assume that the magic would do the same on a mate who wasn't the same werespecies?" she asked accusingly.

She could feel her anger rising disproportionately to anything she had ever felt before. Inside, she could feel the War Elephant ready to go nuclear. The more Ansel and the impundulu fell into despair about their people, the madder she became. Imani wasn't sure when it had happened, maybe from the beginning yesterday, but the War Elephant had decided the entire Rare and Unknowns were Herd.

Her Herd.

She felt punched in the gut. All the air left her lungs. The weight of two million souls bent her shoulders forward like Atlas. All the responsibility she had run from in Atlanta was here and twenty times greater than she ever imagined being a part of as a Herd.

Imani snapped back from the realization to hear the Seer had gone off on a familiar subject. She'd overheard many conversations, debates and outright screaming phone arguments between her grandmother and the Seer. "You elephants are so damn secretive! We don't even know what magic powers you possess or how they work. You won't let us test you. Hell, we don't even know how many War Elephants there have been."

"I think my grandmother has been perfectly clear that we are not going to submit to being magical guinea pigs for you to test us to find the extent of our magical immunity."

"Yes, I have," Seraphine said with finality from the doorway.

Imani and Ansel both scrambled to their feet. Seraphine filled the entire floor with her presence. Ansel felt her Alpha powers bending him to submit, to bow, to take a knee, to prostrate himself before her. Fighting Seraphine's power to continue standing and not submit triggered a migraine in Ansel's left temple. Sharp pains radiated from his temple down the thick column of his neck and into his back.

The mating bond throbbed giving Ansel instant relief from the pain of Seraphine's colossal presence. He still felt woozy and disoriented. Suddenly, he was falling down toward the conference table.

"Grandmother!" Imani shouted.

Seraphine, Imani and Joseph all reached to catch the fainting Ansel before he fell through the conference room table.

"Pull your powers in! Ansel is extremely susceptible right now to magic," Imani shouted. The War Elephant shoved her magic through the mating bond trying to bolster his defenses.

With a Herculean effort, Seraphine begin the task of tucking in her enormous powers. She hadn't even attempted to stop herself from radiating power outwards in months, no years. The entire time that Seraphine worked, Imani pulsed healing powers into the bond between herself and Ansel. While Ansel said nothing, she felt him in pain as every wave of her grandmother's power crested over him.

The Seer and the rest of the Herd said nothing. As everyone filed into the magically expanding room. The round cheap conference table that had been set for three morphed into a long, burnished mahogany rectangle that could have graced the boardrooms of any Fortune 100 company. Chairs begin filling in the gap providing seating for the three dozen Herd and the Rare and Unknown security personnel.

"When do we fight?" Aunt Jackie demanded. Imani could see the wheels of her aunt's mind churning out battle plans. "Who do we fight?"

"We aren't here to fight, are we? I thought we were here to escort Imani and Ansel back to Atlanta and the safety of the Herd House," Aunt Janet asked curtly.

Panic flared through Imani as the thought of returning home to the Herd House after fleeing only three weeks previously. She felt like she had barely just escaped the confines of home and shaken off the shackles of Herd life. Tears sprang to her eyes as she imagined living under one roof with a dozen members of her family again.

"I have a nest prepared for my mate. There will be no returning to the Herd House except as a visitor," Ansel said to all assembled. He choked out the words. Barely able to lift his head to stare at anyone. Only his elbows braced against the side of the table held him upright.

Immediately, Imani begin redoubling the healing she was sending through the bond.

Aunt Jackie dismissed his statement with a toss of her hair. "You can barely look after yourself right now. How are you supposed to protect Our Heir?"

"Protection is not always about brute strength," Cheryl answered for her brother. "We have magic users in R and U. My brother has a security team and his home has been fortified to withstand almost any attack! Magical or physical attack." She paused. "Maybe, if the Stewards had bothered to ask us questions before trying to force them out of our home base. We would have shown them the progress we have made since our grandparent's time. No impundulu lives without onion like layers of protection around us."

The Director of the Shifters & Magic Task Wardens walked in a moment later to pure chaos. Behind her, were Special Agents Orozco and Harrellson with four other Special Agents who all stared blankly as the Seer sat at the head of the table, the new couple sat together at the foot and each side was filled in on one side by the Herd and on the side by shifters of the Rare and Unknown all screaming at one another.

The centaur bucked like a rocking horse toy, stomping her double shod hooves against the thinly carpeted floor. The echo of eight magic shod horseshoes striking together sounded like thunder booming in the conference room. It had the needed effect of quickly and effectively silencing the warring sides. Everyone turned to view the topless centaur as she strode into the room and toward the head of the table next to the Seer. A regular conference room chair morphed into a low-slung chaise lounge as the Director approached. She spread across the chaise in a blur.

"I see all the relevant and not so relevant parties have arrived." Her voice was the lightning to her hooves thunder. Sharp, crackling with hints of magic and sparks of energy.

"Agents Orozco and Harrellson, two of our best Agents, tell me that you dismissed them for protecting you yesterday." She addressed the whole room, but her wideset, pupil less eyes bored holes into Ansel and Imani. "It's a shame that you don't want Steward protection because Mahjabeen and her super coven children materialized outside of the building a few moments ago."

"It's also too bad that some of the oldest wards on the building have been stripped off..." the Seer continued, "Especially with our one on duty SWAT team still running for the hills because of the junior WarElephant."

Guilt assailed Imani as she realized the trouble that awaited them outside. If she hadn't been bucking for a fight with the Stewards this morning, then they would have been better prepared for the real war. She turned to look at Ansel. He was holding himself rigid but clearly the amount of magic in the room was affecting him. The mating bond so thick and strong, like cargo ship rope this morning was weak and thinning. She made her decision quickly.

"We seek protection of the Stewards. We don't have the magical firepower," she said softly, explaining to everyone her decision.

Chapter Twenty-Seven
The Greatest Magical Force

*M*ahjabeen stood in the center of a circle of fourteen of her children. Genuine delight flowed through her veins. She had lied and stolen to conceive enough magical children to build her own coven.

These magical children were her pride and joy. Not that she didn't like or even love some of her other children, but these fourteen magic wielders were her greatest achievement – not a complex spell or taking down a rival or even graduating first in magical academy so long ago. Reviving her family's heritage of dark magic and super covens has been her burning desire for the last seventy-five years.

"We are about to become the greatest magical force this world has seen in over a century. No other group on this planet is more maligned than magic users. No other group is barred and limited the way we are. We have the right to gather in whatever numbers we want...the right to practice whatever magic we want!"

She paused, breathless. "Let's go take the Alpha and make magic flourish freely again!"

Chapter Twenty-Eight
Stalling

The sliding glass doors creaked open slowly for the Director, too slowly for the Director's failed patience and mile wide temper. Never in the over three-hundred year history of the once very hidden and very secretive organization had the bad guys stormed the Headquarters of the Shifters and Magic Task Wardens. Even the worst shifter and hardened magic criminals avoided this building.

Yet, here was an entire family of witches outside her doors. An illegal super coven assembled and making demands that she releases the R & U Alpha to them. They must be insane if they assumed she would just hand over her own Alpha and the rest of her Ageli to them.

Her double shod hooves disconcertingly rang against the concrete. It was the only man-made noise outside, accompanied by the slow moving whoosh of the Trinity River on its lazy circuit of the building.

"You will yield to me," Zosime demanded as she looked down on the diminutive witch. Stopping just four feet away from the coven line. Mahjabeen was maybe four feet eleven, slightly stooped with a small rounded hump in the way of the truly elderly. Her white hair was limp, thin wisps across her skull. Zosime could see the lighter walnut skin of her skull through her hair. What Mahjabeen lacked in size she more than made up for in magical ability. Just like shifters, witches and warlocks got more powerful as they aged. No one knew Mahjabeen's exact age, but there were references to her in the

Steward files going back over one hundred and twelve years.

Zosime felt exposed. She knew that there were six Agent Shifter sharpshooters setting up on the roof. Their long guns would be sighted on the coven and not at her. A dozen magic trained Agent Witches waiting in the destroyed lobby to run to her aid. Their battle magic primed and ready to subdue. Another dozen Agent Witches chanting the building protection spells and wards back into place. They would have a place of safety to retreat if they needed.

She had sounded the alarm to all the field offices. More Steward Agents were pouring in from New Orleans, Miami, New York, Los Angeles and all the North American cities as fast as they could line up to step through the portals. The overseas offices were channeling raw power into blocks the size of shipping containers to be teleported in to replenish Agents if or when they drained their magical reserves.

All that backup wasn't going to help her at this moment as she stood alone in front of the family coven of fifteen. Their magic would resonate together and multiply exponentially. With Mahjabeen directing all of her hatred and the combined forces of their magic, they would be an unfathomable foe.

"You will yield to me," she repeated. No sign of weakness or waver in her voice. Sixty years working as a Steward, twenty of them undercover had given Zosime the ability to be cool under pressure even if her knees and heart were knocking.

"We will not yield, Centaur. Give us the Alpha and we will leave," Mahjabeen declared. "Otherwise, we will level this building and take him."

"You've gone feeble in your dotage if you think we will surrender to you and your rag tag coven of spineless children," Zosime declared. "Shouldn't you be in a nursing home or hospice somewhere or playing with your great-great-great grandchildren? This is foolish on your part and dragging down your whole line."

The five warlocks all bristled at her words. Nine witches ignored her. She realized the witches were the true power source to what she felt sprinkling over her skin. The nine were chanting a spell together. She needed to break their concentration. She had witnessed smaller covens work complicated magic before and that magic failed because of a toddler grabbing its mother around the knee.

The men were there for numbers. She had to stall longer hoping that enough Agents Witches, Shifter, Warlocks, could get here in time to help forestall the coming battle. In the meantime, she needed to break the witches' concentration.

Zosime's back hooves begin tapping counterpoint to the witch's rhythm. She was going to have to break out her Eleanor Powell and Savion Glover impressions.

Chapter Twenty-Nine

Not Enough Magic

"**I**s she tap dancing?" Imani asked the room. She felt trapped. They were in the same conference room with the rest of the Herd and Ansel's family and R & U Security.

The Seer had done something with her hand. Not the quick throwing of fingers, the flick most magic users utilized, but more like a jazz finger instead of jazz hand. Whatever the motion, the wall was now a giant screen where they could see the Director standing all alone facing down a threat that was here for Ansel and her.

"Stalling tactic until more Agents get here," her Aunt Jackie surmised. Watching the centaur Director tap dance like she wished she had a bucket of popcorn to go with the show.

Imani inwardly chuckled at her aunt's blasé attitude. Anyone who knew Jackie, knew she would rather be outside cracking heads than sitting at a table while someone else fought a battle for the Herd.

"How long does it take for an Agent to teleport?" someone asked. They all sat or stood staring at the wall, willing the coven to leave or surrender.

"Five minutes to push an Agent through the portal," Orozco answered.

"Ten minutes for that Agent to recover." the Seer finished.

"Too long," Imani and elephant concluded together. She turned to see Ansel slumping down in his chair with his head cradled in his arms, resting on the conference table. The 'phant had been pushing energy through the bond steadily for what seemed like hours now. Ansel showed no signs of getting better. He was worse. She opened up her awareness fully. Giving her a view of all the magic surrounding her. This was the key to the War Elephant's magical immunity. They could see the magic in the air like normal people saw rainbows and cut it magically from the root. Ansel and she were connected by the mating bond which last night had strengthened to the thickness of a Buick station wagon. Under her scrutiny, it looked like someone was carving chunks out of the bond. Awareness hit her dead in the face as she realized that there was another bond from Ansel to the coven outside. They were stripping the soul out of him. Could they take him from her even without his body?

If they captured his spirit, his body would be sure to follow of its own volition. She pictured his grandparents, Laibon and Naserian held as magical slaves for over a decade forced to kill at the whims of others. That would not happen to Ansel or her or any of the Rare and Unknown ever!

They couldn't wait for the coven to surrender. They didn't seem receptive to negotiations if the Director was out there literally tap dancing. Realization dawned as she watched the magical glow of their mating bond dim faster. The coven didn't really expect the Stewards to surrender Ansel to them, they were just here to drain him magically.

Imani couldn't tell if it was hers or if it was the War Elephant's decision, but she felt her body move backwards to the far side of the narrow conference room. Kicking off her heels, she ran full speed toward the closest window of the room. Crashing through the double paned window, she shifted from human to War Elephant as she plummeted four stories to the ground below.

The War Elephant landed on the thin strip of landscaping that surrounded the Steward's Headquarters. Some type of spiked drought resistant shrubbery lay crushed under her right hind foot. Her adrenaline was pumping, the needles didn't even penetrate the armor of her feet. Another shrub was tickling her nether regions. Dirt and grass were under her left feet. Her right front foot had caved in the concrete sidewalk.

Mentally, she picked her targets. The WarElephant powers allowed her to mark them magically. Her very own magic tracking system. If they escaped today, she could follow them across the planet. No amount of magic would keep them from escaping her wrath.

Fifteen enemies. She wanted the mother, Mahjabeen first. If she cut off the head of the beast, the rest of the body died.

The witches and the centaur were all staring open mouthed at her flying entrance. With one mighty heave, she lifted her foot from the cave she had created.

All of her weapons were out, triple tusks, armored marble hide, mace tipped tail. Her magic was circulating one inch above her armor like a moving bubble wrap. It would disperse any light battle magics thrown at her. She was ready to rampage.

She was ready for battle.

"The Alpha is mine!" she bellowed for all the world to hear. Her voice clear to every ear within ten miles. Head thrown all the way back she trumpeted her battle cry. She charged the line of witches heading for the center and hopefully the most powerful witches.

She hit the coven line like a bowling ball hurled from the hands of a drunk frat boy. She crushed one warlock underfoot when he got between her and the old woman. She heard the sounds of his bones breaking like the noise from a distant room. Fourteen targets.

As she charged forward to chase another witch to her death, something like a weighted net landed on her. The weight of the magic held her in place.

"Mother we need to leave now! The Stewards aren't going to just keep waiting for the centaur to negotiate. She's just a stalling tactic!" one of the witches yelled from nearby.

"I need more time. The impundulu's soul can be ours. His body will follow," the creaky old witch yelled back.

"If the spell was going to work it would have done so by now. Evelyn marked him wrong."

Another young witch yelled, "We need to leave now!"

Imani felt more magic stirring into the winds of a teleportation spell. Imani redoubled her efforts to free herself from the net. They weren't about to activate some back up escape plan with her within feet of them. She shook herself all over like a wet dog shaking water out of its fur. She was shaking the magic that was clinging to her. Mentally, she was pushing back against the weight holding her in place. Her magic strained and flexed.

The magical net holding her broke all at once and the spell rebounded on its casters. Four witches and warlocks collapsed to the ground like a quartet of puppets with their strings severed by a giant hand. Eleven targets.

Imani felt all of the ozone disappear from the atmosphere. The mating bond pulsed with reassurance. She turned back toward the building in time to see Ansel then Cheryl leap from the fifth-floor window and transform into impundulus. Their combined wingspans blacking out the blue sky above as they flew together toward her. Her body hummed from tip to tail as she felt her mate and his twin charge their lightning. Together, the twins launched four bolts, one from each wing tip, toward the collapsing line of the coven. Imani felt one of the witch's mind snap as the lightning struck her. Ten targets.

The lightning birds rocketed past them, like fighter jets they were in tight formation. Wingtips inches apart as they flew veering in opposite directions.

Around her chaos ensued as more of the coven threw wild dark green battle magic like machine gun fire at the charging line of Agent Witches, a dozen Herd members in battle form standing on two feet and trumpeting their personal battle cries and the assortment of Rare and Unknown shifters from Ansel's security team who all burst from the building launched from a cannon of impatience.

The centaur stood tall bellowing orders to take the downed witches into custody. In her fist, Zosime held a struggling warlock three feet off the ground as he took wild swings at her face or breasts. None of his punches landed, every time he swung at her she just shook him like a rattle. From ten feet away, Imani could see the warlock was so dizzy, if the centaur dropped him, he wouldn't be able to stand for more than one moment. Nine targets.

Mahjabeen stood alone, unmoving in the chaos as she chanted. "A soul for a soul. A life for a life. A soul for a soul. A life for a life. A soul for a soul. A life for a life." Imani watched the souls of her dead children who littered the battlefield rise. "Let those bearing my mark return to my service. Let those bearing my mark return to my service. Let those bearing my mark return to my service." Between her outstretched fingers a sickening black orb formed, the souls of her deceased children lined up joining into the magic working between her hands. The orb pulsed as the souls of Mahjabeen's three children were sucked into the miasma of dark magic.

"Bring the soul of the Alpha to me and I'll resurrect you. Fail me and I'll torment your afterlife." Mahjabeen instructed the orb. She funneled more magic into the orb.

Just looking in its direction, Imani felt the wrongness of it. It gave her nausea. Imani felt the orb's sentience. It was the worst type of death magic. Forcing the souls of the dead to be of service to the living. This coven needed to be destroyed inside out and outside in. They could never be allowed to resemble; family or not, they were corrupt.

Imani's magic reached for the orb. She would tear it apart molecule by molecule freeing the souls and destroying the magic contained within. The slightest touch of her powers to the orb made her ill; it even felt slimy and oily to her magic like dirty dishwater. There were magical things being pulled into the orb's vortex that she couldn't identify. She reached harder this time trying to pull it away from the witch. The orb came toward her one foot, two foot, three; then careened out of her reach closer to Mahjabeen.

She had to smash the fiber of that black magic before it undid everything. Again, Imani felt Ansel and Cheryl charging for another strike. The sky flashed white temporarily blinding the entire field.

Just as the twin impundulus' lightning bolts struck, the last warlock grabbed Mahjabeen in his arms. He cradled her gently one arm below her knees and one across her back, but the winds of the teleport spell swirled the thin wisps of her hair. The ancient crone released her black orb and it flew directly upward and toward Ansel as he came flying past.

Rushing forward, Imani tried to snake her trunk around the pair of them, but she came back with dark magic tinged air. Her trunk burned like she'd been splashed with acid.

The black orb struck Ansel directly in the chest. Imani's heart stopped. Her breath caught in her chest. Her whole world narrowed as she felt the mating bond severed cleanly from between them. She stood dumbfounded as the impundulu shifted back to Ansel and begin plummeting fifty feet down.

She thundered across the parking lot to where he was falling. Seraphine had once told her that if the War Elephant could imagine it, she could do it. Imani imagined her powers forming into a giant baseball glove.

She smashed three cars in her urgency to be there before Ansel landed. The impact of his landing caused tremors across the parking lot. Imani shifted back to human. Dropping to her knees, she picked up his broken body and cradled him to her chest. There was no movement she could see in his face. She didn't hear his heart beating.

He was gone before she had a chance to tell him she loved him. Before they were able to get married and have babies and spend the rest of their lives together. He couldn't be gone.

"No. No. No. No. No," she chanted. She wanted to rip out her own heart and stick it in his chest.

Tears streamed uncontrollably from her eyes blurring her vision. It wasn't until her grandmother's trunk touched her shoulder and Seraphine whispered, "Push your magic out of you and into him."

"What?"

"Push all your magic out of you and into him. It's how I saved your grandfather during the War. Push all of it, don't leave any in you. It'll hurt like hell, but you'll have your man back. You won't be able to shift or fight or anything for a while. I couldn't shift for two years, but it was two years as a human with your grandfather."

Imani wiped the tears from her face. They kept streaming from her eyes uncontrollably. She placed Ansel gently back on the cracked and uneven asphalt of the parking lot. The ground was littered with wreckage from the fight taking place around them. She could see little kernels of unshaped magic that had sloughed off during hasty spell casting.

She felt the War Elephant release her control as Imani gathered every bit of magic in her body. There was no hesitation she would be human for the rest of her life if it meant spending it as Ansel's wife.

Cheryl landed next to them. "Ansel!" she screamed. She tried to grab her twin's body, but Imani and Seraphine stopped her. "Leave him alone!"

Imani hadn't even thought of Cheryl. After the Centumrogatio she knew Ansel loved his twin more than himself and vice versa.

"My grandmother says we can save him."

"Get away from him!" Cheryl screamed. She was on the verge of hysteria; tears streamed from her face, her breathing was ragged. "Our bond is gone! I felt it cut clean." She fisted her hands at her side. Imani could see her temper building. "He'd be alive if he hadn't chased your ass out here."

"I'm going to bring him back!" Imani yelled, but Cheryl was lost in her grief.

Imani turned back to her mate. She didn't see the blow coming.

Cheryl slammed her entire body into Imani's spine. Imani had at least sixty to seventy pounds on Cheryl, but the blow knocked her off of her feet. She scrapped her hands and knees across the parking lot. Seraphine shifted to human, grabbing Cheryl off of Imani.

"Hurry, Imani, don't wait too long or he won't be able to be resurrected!" Grandmother yelled, as she slapped Cheryl across the face. A distraught Cheryl burst into tears.

Imani pushed every gram of magic from her body. She said goodbye to shifting forever. She said goodbye to her life with the Herd. The rest of her life she would spend as a human if this worked. This has to work, she prayed to every god and goddess that she had ever heard of.

A blue white orb formed between her hands. She placed it gently onto the jagged hole where Mahjabeen's orb had struck him.

They watched as his body begin to absorb her innate magic. He spasmed on the ground. Once.

Twice.

Imani turned to her grandmother. "What now?"

"I don't know. That was it before!"

Cheryl reached forward and pushed a purple nebula ball of energy on top of Imani's orb. Together, the orbs combined and sunk deeper into Ansel. The ragged whole in his chest begin to repair itself, muscle by muscle and bone by bone. Even to Imani's now regular human ears, she could hear his bones repairing themselves.

Chapter Thirty

Man Has To Be Quick

Imani and Cheryl sat together on the narrow bench. They said nothing to one another. Between them on the narrow bench, the two held hands. They had not moved for the last few days; just sat watching Ansel's monitors.

Members of the Herd and R & U had streamed in and out, offering to relieve the two but neither had managed to be gone longer than a trip to the bathroom. Constant worry over Ansel had formed an uneasy trucc between them over the last few days but they were far from being friends.

The white haired, white eyed Steward doctor came in and both women stood. He was followed closely by Kathleen, Josephine, Seraphine and Zosime.

"Are you sure?" Zosime asked the doctor again. The Centaur looked like she had questioned the doctor several times.

"What if he wakes up with Mahjabeen's magic still in him? What if waking him up reactivates the magic?" The Steward Director asked again.

"Stop being a worrywart, Zosime." The Seer trailed in after everyone. She was wrapped head to toe in red. Everyone else was wearing Steward issued navy blue scrubs. No one had wanted to leave the Headquarters building even to travel to the store for clothing.

"Yes, Director. I'm positive. We don't need to keep him in a medically induced coma any longer. His vital signs are steady, there's no swelling, no brain damage. No magical pathogens or viruses or tracers. There is nothing magical attacking him. The junior War Elephant's magic has healed everything. Killed everything magical. His shifter healing has repaired everything. There is no medical magic I can work that hasn't already been done by these two." He gestured to Imani and Cheryl.

He pulled a syringe out of the pocket of his blue lab coat. He plunged the syringe into Ansel's IV line.

The group stood watching.

Twelve minutes passed, but no one moved. On side of the bed nearest the door, stood the Doctor. Cheryl and Imani stood vigil on the left side of the bed. At the foot, Seraphine, Josephine and Kathleen waited.

Ansel opened his eyes. His eyes searched the group looking for one face. He struggled to sit up. Kathleen found the button on the side of the bed's railing and pushed until Ansel was in a seated position.

Groggily he said, "This isn't really how I wanted to ask you to marry me, Princess, but a man has to be quick with you or you'll outrun him."

Imani's eyes let loose six days' worth of tears as she went to his bedside. "Shouldn't there be a question in there?"

Grabbing her hand, Ansel asked quietly. "Imani Seraphine Wilson, will you make the rest of my life as interesting as the last three weeks by becoming my wife?"

"Maybe?" she gave him a sphinxlike smile.

"Maybe, woman?" Ansel's voice went up an octave.

"Do I still get a million orgasms and your undying love and devotion?"

"Yes." He chuckled. "All my undying love and devotion plus a million orgasms."

"Yes." She chuckled back.

Lagniappe

I hope you enjoyed your journey into the world of the Rare and Unknowns and Ansel and Imani's adventure. Their story continues in a between the numbers novella, The Crutchfields and The McNamaras. Cheryl's story The Shifter Bachelorette where you will meet new hot Alpha shifters and the Alphas who love them. I hope you enjoy reading it as much as I have enjoyed writing it. If you would like the recipes from Henrietta's Alpha fest, join my newsletter list here.

Feel free to join The Rare and The Unknown Facebook group, everyone is super friendly.

Keep reading for a preview of The Shifter Bachelorette on sale now.

The Bachelor Series
The Shifter Bachelor
The Shifter Bachelorette
Bachelorette in Heat
Bachelor in Trouble
Bachelorette on a Mission – Coming October 2019
Bachelor in Paradise – Coming December 2019

Between the Numbers
The Crutchfields and The McNamaras
Trouble Ex Machina
Shorts
The After Market, Volume 1
The After Market, Volume 2

Social Aid & Pleasure

Acknowledgments

Writing is a sport and just like any athlete, I have a team of amazing people supporting me on the field and off.

All thanks to my daughter, G.A.P better known as Flamingo Legs, who let me bounce ideas off of her and allowed me to watch her read pages just to see her facial expressions.

More thanks to my Alpha reader, Rameisha Haqq-Johnson who may be my biggest fan and vice president of my fan club.

My Beta readers who are too numerous to name but are just as crucial and influential to me.

Most of my grammar and punctuation faux pas were viciously corrected by Urania Fung and all the members of the Northeast Arlington Writers' Critique Group and by my editor, Elizabeth.

The Shifter Bachelorette:

A Rare and Unknown Romance

Book Two

Cheryl held her breath as her brother's mate replied sarcastically, "I must have suffered hearing loss during the night. Did you just say you wanted to turn our wedding into a televised special?" She clutched the desk phone tighter to her ear as she waited for her brother to work his magic on the cranky War Elephant.

"Dexter and my mother and even Cheryl think it's a fabulous idea. Our wedding will be the lead in special for the new Shifter Bachelor show they've been pitching. Princess, I think you forget how famous your family is sometimes. Just the mention of your grandmother's name and the networks started a bidding war for the show," Ansel said charmingly.

Imani said nothing.

After a few seconds of tense silence, her brother switched tactics. "Think of all the single Alpha shifters I have under me, who are struggling to maintain a decent lifestyle for themselves and their people like the MacBhaird family. Think of all the businesses we are trying to build and promote. We have an opportunity to expand exponentially here. Having a show with our best single good looking shifters, dating and hopefully mating at our resorts and properties. Our shifters and our products showcased on worldwide television."

Cheryl sighed, Ansel's people, The Rare and Unknowns were her people too. She was Ansel's first Beta. He often called her the Alpha Beta. She wondered for a moment if she had been the first born twin how their lives would be different, but Ansel was fond of telling anyone who would listen that he *wasn't actually born first, Cheryl pushed him out first...*

Imani finally spoke after what seemed like an eternity. "Fine, we'll have a televised wedding ceremony, but it has to be up to Herd standards for dignity and decorum. No asking my grandmother to back that thang up on national television for kicks during the reception."

Cheryl's heart leaped in her chest and gratitude for her twin's mate warmed her heart. They were going to keep so many of their shifters from suffering the ill effects of poverty. Following Dexter Waycross' advice, each shifter who was a member of the R and U was now a shareholder in the shifter owned umbrella company.

"First, we are thinking it will be international television with more like weeks of wedding events." Cheryl couldn't help herself. She tried to contain her excitement as she started explaining to Imani everything she and Dexter had envisioned after the first pitch meeting with the network executives. "We'd want to do the whole thing – ring shopping, gown fittings, bachelor and bachelorette parties, bridesmaids' selection, cake tasting, everything, not just the actual ceremony and reception."

"We want everyone to get a glimpse of the shifter life – the glamorous side, not the ratchet side of people shifting in rage or fighting in cages or acting a fool," Kathleen, her mother, interjected quickly. She always focused on what things would look like not the practical side of things.

Imani paused, and Cheryl could hear the hesitation return. "We have to call my mother. She would need to have final say in the Herd's participation."

"Can we call her now?" Dexter asked. Dexter Waycross, Alpha of the Marshall, Texas werewolf pack and spearhead of most of the new business ideas that Ansel and the executive team were trying to create for their one point seven million shifters. "The quicker we get her permission, the more planning we can do to sell the networks a finished product and show them exactly what kind of access they will be getting into the secret lives of elephants and the rare and unknown shifters."

Imani rattled off her mother, Josephine's cell number while Cheryl both dialed the number and scribbled the number in her planner.

A breathy, "This is Josephine Trudeau," answered on the third ring.

Cheryl sat back and looked to the ceiling slipping the receiver in the crook of her neck, so she could cross the fingers of both hands.

It had been six months since Imani had mated with Ansel and their relationship had turned her orderly world upside down. Her brother had gone into full on mating frenzy for over five and a half months. He had neglected everything from his political science classes at Wiley College, to his duties as Alpha to the Rare and Unknowns and to the duty Cheryl relied on him the most for keeping their mother on the straight and narrow path of not interfering with other people's lives. All his day to day duties had fallen to her in the interim. Cheryl was so glad to see Ansel and Imani out of the bedroom and back to work.

Imani started explaining, "Mother, you are on conference call with me, Ansel, Cheryl, Kathleen and Dexter Waycross. They are pitching a television show to the networks and were led to believe it will sell better if the lead in show was Ansel and my wedding special. I said of course, but that everything would have to be done to Herd decorum standards."

Josephine was quiet so long that Cheryl and the other conference call participants thought she had hung up. "Does this mean we get to have a big free wedding?" There was nothing Josephine Trudeau loved more than the word "free."

"Uh, I guess so." Imani relaxed knowing that free went further to convincing her mother than any other word or deed could.

"Yes, big and free, Mrs. Trudeau," Dexter Waycross promised. "The networks would gladly pay for any and all expenses. If they don't, the production company will cover it."

"Do they really want to see Imani and Ansel's wedding or are they just looking to get Mother on television?"

Mother to Josephine and grandmother to Imani was Seraphine, the War Elephant and the heroine of the Great Shifter War. Seraphine was notoriously camera shy and actively avoided publicity and paparazzi like a germaphobe avoids fast food dumpsters in July.

"To be perfectly honest, Ansel and Imani are the main attraction, but Seraphine is the icing on the cake. Especially if she would consent to do a couple of interviews about the wedding or recount some amusing tidbit about Imani as a child," Cheryl said quickly.

She had seen how fast an elephant could decide; a decision they would be unmoved from after their mind was made up. You had to keep supplying information while they were processing their thoughts. Her experience around Imani and the Marshall Herd were serving her well with negotiations.

"Ansel and my grandmother will be doing the same things that Seraphine will be asked. She is looking forward to telling embarrassing stories about how Ansel got the nickname Antsy."

She heard her twin groan, a low rumble that made everyone on the line chuckle.

Josephine sighed dramatically. "I'm sure it will be ok with the rest of the Herd, but Mother is a different kettle of fish. We have to ask her directly."

Cheryl almost threw the headset of the phone. She had heard that elephants made decisions by committee, but that was seriously getting in the way of her planning this wedding and television special. Luckily, she heard Imani rattling off that phone number before the phone left her hand. She spent a busy couple of seconds dialing the matriarch War Elephant into the conference call and scribbling her personal cell number in her planner. Looking at her planner, she scrambled into her handbag pulling out her personal cell. There was no way she was going to miss the opportunity to put the most famous shifter on the planet's private cell number in her phone.

"I don't buy from telemarketers." was the first thing Seraphine said.

Imani shouted into the phone, "Grandmother it's me, Imani! Don't hang up!"

"Imani?" Seraphine sounded confused for a moment. "Why are you calling me from a strange number?"

"We are on a conference call with Mother, Ansel, his mother and sister and Dexter Waycross."

"Well, I guess this isn't a friendly call to tell me you miss me and Grandpa?" Seraphine said brusquely.

Cheryl's heart froze mid beat as her blood chilled five degrees. Unsure if the Matriarch War Elephant was angry or not. Elephants treated sarcasm as a tertiary language to English. They didn't have a regular sense of humor. Normal jokes didn't even register fleeting smiles.

She had seen both women fight in a battle, hell she had started a fight with them, and her inner animals were definitely not upholding one off, much less both of the War Elephants. She waited cautiously for Imani to explode in anger or laughter.

"Of course, I miss Grandpa," Imani teased her grandmother. "Actually, we're calling you because Ansel's people want to televise our wedding to try and raise money for the Rare and Unknows. The tv networks will pay more if the infamous Seraphine was at her favorite granddaughter's wedding and told embarrassing stories of her childhood."

Seraphine scoffed. "Are you talking about yourself? Favorite granddaughter my ass. I have become quite fond of Itzel. She's a delight and hasn't ignored me for five months while she was practicing getting pregnant with that lighting bird..."

Cheryl muted her phone, so she could laugh completely. *Practicing getting pregnant!* She internally and externally howled with laughter. She'd have to let slip in conversation that her twin and Imani had broken three headboards in five months. She couldn't wait to watch how the Matriarch dropped that bomb into her conversational melee.

Cheryl unmuted her phone just in time to hear the Matriarch give her full blessing and consent to participate in all the wedding activities and even one and only one interview. She listened as everyone gave their individual thanks to Seraphine. The elephants dropped off of the call leaving just herself, Ansel, their mother and Dexter. "I'm sure Cheryl has made like a dozen lists of everything that will need to be done. Just send me my list. I'm going to practice getting my mate pregnant. Practice makes perfect." Ansel disconnected laughing the whole time.

Soon after, her own mother left echoing Ansel's sentiment of delegating the responsibility of creating an overall plan to Cheryl. Dexter too made excuses that he had Pack duties. Just like always, Cheryl found herself at the end holding the bulk of the responsibility to make things happen.

Book Club Discussion Questions

Special thanks to the A.B.L.E. Book club of Oklahoma City, Oklahoma for allowing me to test drive these questions when they invited me to speak.

1. What did you like best about The Shifter Bachelor? _________

____

____

____

____

____

2. What did you like least about The Shifter Bachelor? _______

____

____

____

____

____

3. What other books did this book remind you of? ___________

____

____

____

____

____

4. What authors do you find the world building in The Shifter Bachelor similar too? _______________________________

____

____

____

____

5. Beyond Twilight and any Ann Rice books, have you ever read paranormal romances before? What stopped you from reading them? _______________________________

____

____

____

____

6. What do you consider are the dynamics of Ansel and Imani's relationship? _______________________________

____

____

____

____

7. How do you feel their interactions would play out in the real world? Starting from the coffee shop through to the final chapter? _______________________________

____

____

____

____

8. Would you consent to compete in a Bachelor type dating situation to find a spouse? _______________________________

____

____

____

____

Would you want to win a potential spouse in a reality competition?

____

____

____

____

9. What line of dialogue or sentence spoke directly to you? __

10. What artist would you choose to illustrate this book? What kinds of illustrations would you include? _______________

11. Bonus: Would you watch this book and others in the series as a movie or television series? _______________

Lagniappe About the Author

Shai August is a country girl with a big imagination, more than a touch of wanderlust and a never-ending desire to live in both an RV traveling the world and a library.

Her love language is words of affirmations followed by books, bacon and bourbon.

She's a born and bred Louisiana native, but is currently doing an impression of a yellow rose of Texas. She is fluent in English, sarcasm and memes.

Her goal is to write fast paced, character driven paranormal fiction for women of color.

She's found all over the internet and social media as @ShaiAugust (Facebook, Instagram, Pinterest (*author assumes no responsibility for your falling into her Pinterest board traps*), Twitter, etc.) feel free to follow and start any kind of conversation with me.

Contact directly via email at ShaiAugustWrites@gmail.com

If you would like to join my newsletter list, go here: http://eepurl.com/dI8TSr

Feel free to join The Rare and The Unknown Facebook group, everyone is super friendly, there are sneak peaks of my writing, giveaways and memes.

https://www.facebook.com/groups/403262163476758